"Brilliant novel...one of the most captivating crime mysteries I have read recently."

~Olga Markova for Readers' Favorite

"Touching and relatable...beyond my expectations."

~Mary Clarke for Readers' Favorite

"Compulsive...I loved *Ripple Effect*!"

~Lucinda E. Clarke for Readers' Favorite

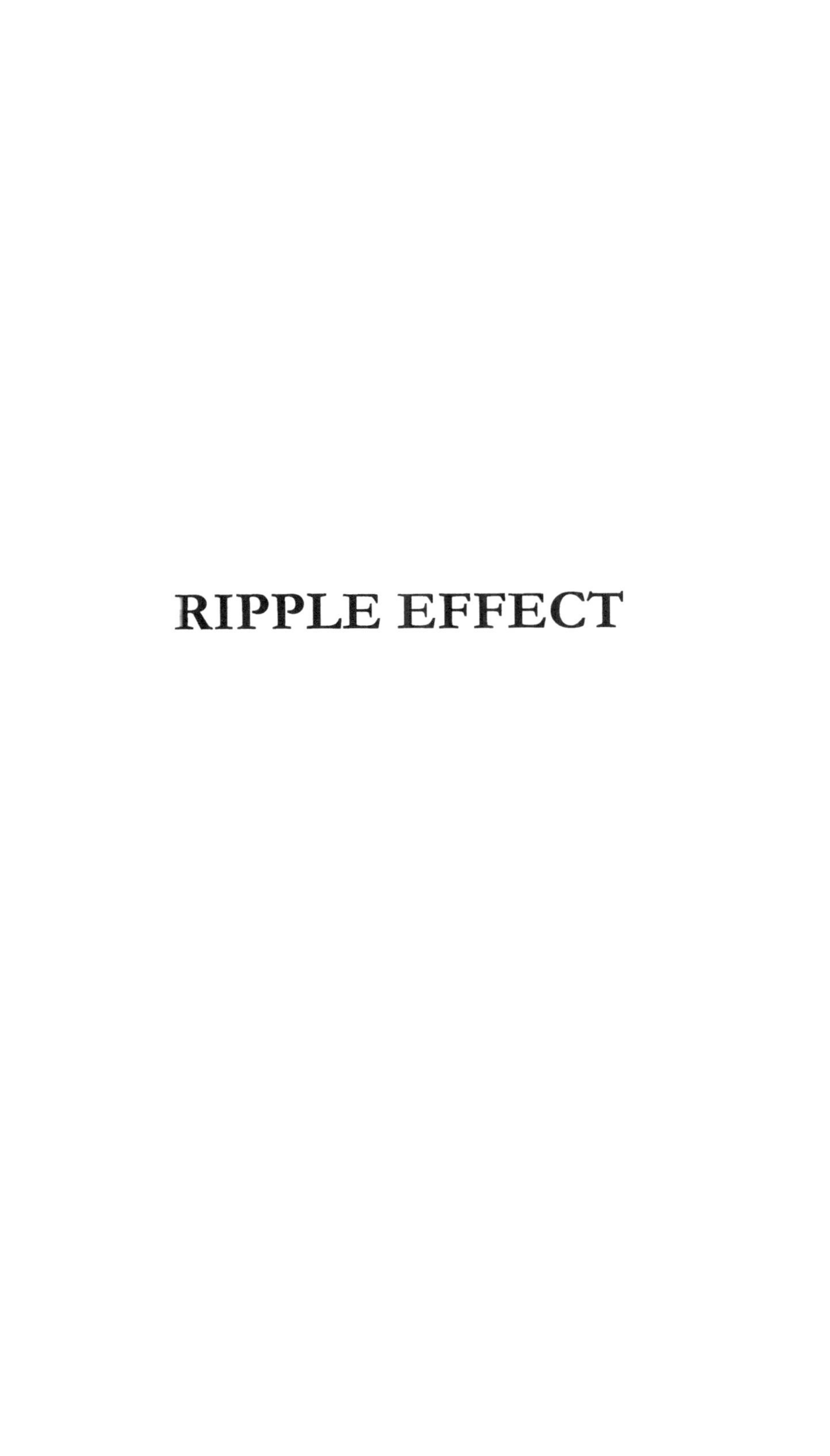

RIPPLE EFFECT

ALSO AVAILABLE BY BRENDA LYNE

<u>NOVELS</u>

Charlie's Mirror

Sister Lost

The Thirteenth Cabin: A Raegan O'Rourke Mystery

Angel Baby: A Raegan O'Rourke Mystery

Fool's Gold: A Raegan O'Rourke Mystery

<u>SHORT STORY COLLECTIONS</u>

Bourbon & Burlap

RIPPLE EFFECT

BRENDA LYNE

Cover design by Susan@yuneepix.com
Book design by Jennifer DeVries

Published in the United States by Brenda Lyne Books

Printed in the United States

ISBN: 979-8-9903715-4-5

First edition: September 2025

brendalyne.com

For Annette.

It still doesn't quite feel real.

Thank you. For everything.

PROLOGUE:
THE DEAD GIRL

2008

A heavy thud, punctuated by the muted crunch of snapping twigs and the soft rustle of displaced foliage, jars me awake. I look wildly around, trying to get my bearings, until shadowy movement catches my attention. It's a person, walking away from me as quickly as the dense underbrush of the forest will allow. They wear jeans and a dark-colored t-shirt, and their heavy footfalls are muffled by a thick carpet of leaves as they push through ferns and brambles.

Panic crashes in and I try to cry out: *Wait! Come back! Where am I? How did I get here? Who are you?* But my voice won't work. I don't make any sound at all. What is wrong with me?

Leaves rustle and branches crack as the person – man or woman, I can't tell – rounds the trunk of a huge old oak tree and disappears. The cracks and rustles slowly fade…and then, silence. It's thick silence, broken only by the whisper of the breeze in the treetops, and it wraps around me like a blanket.

Now that I'm alone, the panic recedes enough that I can assess my situation. First, the obvious: I'm deep in a dense forest, surrounded by tree trunks and broken branches and scrub brush. Sunlight pokes through the forty-foot leaf canopy, casting tiny beams like a disco ball. The only other living things besides me are the birds and the squirrels, who have gone back to their daily business.

There's something fundamentally wrong here, though. My point of view, the way I see and observe my surroundings, has…changed somehow. It's like my peripheral vision has expanded infinitely, and I'm not limited to the tunnel of my eyes anymore. I see…*more*.

What is going on?

I shift my view from the trees above to the ground below – and I'm rocked to my very core by what I see there.

The teenaged girl's body lying on the forest floor is mine. I don't know how I know this, but I do. There's no question. The body may be mine, but it's clearly not *me*. Not anymore. My soul, my essence, what made me who I am has left it, leaving behind a lifeless shell. The eyes are half closed, staring at nothing. A swollen tongue pokes out between blue lips. Angry red marks decorate the neck. Curly brown hair is pulled back in a messy ponytail. The white t-shirt, stained with blood, is dirty. A silver charm bracelet hangs on one limp arm.

Holy shit. I'm dead. I'm fucking *dead*.

The panic creeps back. How in the hell did this happen? Did the person I saw walking away have something to do with it? I try to remember, and I'm promptly hit by a tsunami of pure electric terror. And then, as if that isn't fun enough, invisible hands seize my throat and squeeze. The alarming sensation (*If I'm dead, how can I be choking?*) brings the panic back in full force. Oh my god oh my god I can't *breathe*.

I retreat, and the fear and pain subside. The pressure on my throat eases. All memories of my life and death stay maddeningly out of reach. I don't know how I lived, how I died, where I am, how I got here…I don't even know my name.

Great. Now what do I do?

There's not much I can do, I guess. I'm stuck here with a dead person's version of amnesia until someone finds my body.

I hope they find me quickly.

They don't. The sun rises and sets, winds and rains come and go, and days pass. I don't know how many days. I learn pretty quickly that when you're dead, the concept of time is irrelevant. I go nowhere, I do nothing, and seconds, minutes, hours, days, weeks, months, or years simply don't mean anything. All I know is I wait for a very long time.

And I watch. The wildlife are kind of entertaining; squirrels chatter, chase each other up and down the trees, and stuff acorns in their cheeks. Birds do a fluttery dance with each other in midair or perch on nearby branches and sing their songs. Woodpeckers keep a distinct rhythm as they drill holes in the trees with their strong beaks, looking for delicious insects. A herd of white-tailed deer, led by the alpha doe, amble by on their way to find water. The majestic buck with his crown of antlers brings up the rear. Their coats grow thicker and turn redder with every passing day.

The seasons are changing.

The body on the ground is changing too, gradually. The skin turns pale as gravity pulls the blood to the lowest places. Blowflies lay their eggs in the flesh, and the maggots hatch just as bloating and putrefaction set in. Foxes, raccoons, crows, and even nasty beetles feast on rotting flesh, tearing decaying muscle and scattering bones. Any tissues left turn to liquid and soak into the ground. I am literally watching my own body disintegrate and become one with the earth. It's unsettling, and kind of gross.

And no matter how hard I try, I still can't access my memories. The unbearable terror and terrifying choking sensation hit me like a wrecking ball every time, driving me back. I can't break through it. So I finally just stop trying. There's no point in torturing myself.

By the time the first snow falls, I'm losing hope that my remains will ever be found. I'll be stuck here in this random forest forever. Rather than waiting and watching the time go by, I decide to try something different. I shift my view inward and suspend myself in deep and never-ending darkness. It's peaceful here. I imagine it must be like sleeping was when I was alive.

Not that I can remember.

2009

The sweet song of a cardinal finally draws me out of the darkness. Two high-pitched *tweet*s, followed by exactly seven lower-pitched *peer*s, and the pattern repeats over and over again. It's the sound of new life. It's the sound of spring.

The snow has melted away and the trees' green cloaks are growing in. Delicate green shoots poke up from under the layers of dead leaves on the ground and stretch toward the sun, growing around and through whatever's in their path – including my scattered bones. One particularly aggressive little weed is already making its way through the skull, exiting via an eye socket.

Nobody has found me yet, I guess. I don't get it. Doesn't anybody miss me? Hasn't anybody noticed yet that I'm gone? Don't I have a family? How does a teenaged girl end up dead in the woods and nobody's come looking for her? Where are my people?

My frustration is as useless as trying to call up any memories of my life. My past is hidden from me, I'm stuck in the present, and I have no future. And there isn't a damn thing I can do about it. I'm just…here. Is this where I'll be forever? What's keeping me here? Does this happen to everyone when they die?

More questions with no answers. I might as well go back to sleep.

A flash of crimson catches my attention. It's a cardinal, probably the one whose singing woke me up. He lands in a nearby evergreen tree and sings again. He's very handsome, bright red, with a cute little crest on top of his head and a black mask on his face. He's joined by his mate; she is more brown than red but still pretty. They're an adorable couple, and I see soon enough that they're building their nest.

Now that I have neighbors, I think I'll stay awake for a little while and watch them. Maybe I'll even give them names.

Bella…

Edward…

Those two specific names float across my consciousness like helium balloons. I don't know where they came from, but they're perfect for my new feathered friends.

Days pass as I watch Bella and Edward build their nest, lay their eggs, and tend to their young. They're very attentive parents, making sure their babies are fed a steady diet of bugs and spiders. Watching them makes me wonder: did my parents take good care of me? What were they like? Do they miss me?

Bella and Edward's babies are nearly grown when the day I've been waiting for finally arrives. They're little balls of brown feathers, super cute, and Edward takes over parenting duties. While he shows his offspring how to fly, find food, and avoid predators, Bella moves to a different tree and starts building a second nest.

A cardinal parent's work is never done, I guess.

A foreign sound scatters the birds and the entire forest hushes, listening. Yep, there it is again: a tinkling sound, accompanied by rapid trotting footfalls and the swish of dry leaves.

Something's coming. And it's not something that belongs here.

A large German shepherd appears from behind the huge old oak tree. It's a beautiful dog, with a black and tan coat, tall pointy ears, and intelligent eyes. It wears a red collar with SARGE embroidered on it in white letters. A bell attached to the collar jingles as the dog paces and sniffs around the area where my scattered bones lay. It stops, sniffs one spot very closely, then squares up and uses its powerful jaws to lift a long bone off the ground. The weeds entangling the bone snap like guitar strings. One end of the bone is round like a ball, and the other end has two distinct knobs. I don't know how I know this means it's a leg bone, but I do.

"Sarge! Get back here! Come on, boy!" The dog takes off running toward a man's distant voice, the comically long bone firmly clamped in its teeth.

This is good. The dog will bring the bone to its owner, and they'll call the police. Finally, after waiting for so long, I'm going to be found.

The forest is just getting back into its normal rhythm when I hear sirens wailing in the distance. Not long after that, two male voices send the animals back into their hiding spots.

"This way," one man says. "Whoa, hold on, boy."

The dog reappears, this time on a leash, and he's pulling so hard it looks like he's taking his owner for a walk. The owner, a tall elderly man with thinning gray hair, a sharp nose, and round glasses, somehow manages to stay in control. He's followed by a much younger uniformed policeman with sport sunglasses pushed up into his crewcut blond hair and A. BANE embroidered on the right chest pocket of his black shirt.

The dog sits and barks. "I guess this is the spot," the older man says. He's now holding the dog by its collar to keep it in place.

Officer Bane walks a wide perimeter around the area, examining the ground. "Oh. Yeah, here we go." His pants creak as he squats and brushes aside some weeds to reveal another bone. He looks around and points to a round white shape poking up from the groundcover a few feet away. "And that's probably the skull."

The older man nods in agreement.

Officer Bane stands. "Let's head back to the parking lot. I'm going to call our investigations unit and the crime scene team, and then I have to tape off the whole area. If you could stay and talk to the detectives when they get here, that would be great."

"Of course," the older man says. "Whatever I can do to help."

The men head out the way they came in. This time the owner is pulling the dog, which keeps turning and looking longingly back at the bone field. Soon they disappear, and again I wait.

Officer Bane comes back and cordons the area off with yellow crime scene tape. As he's doing that, more people start showing up: a pair of women wearing navy blue DOJ CRIME SCENE jackets carrying what look kind of like oversized tackle boxes, and two men in black shirts with SUPERIOR POLICE embroidered in gold on the left chest.

This is the first time I've seen anything that indicates where I am. Superior? As in Superior, Wisconsin? Is that where I live? It's not ringing a bell, but…maybe?

The detectives – one a big Black man who looks like he spends all of his free time at the gym, the other a tall white guy who looks like he doesn't sleep much – set about examining the scene.

"Nothing but bones," the white guy says. He looks a bit intimidated.

"Yeah, they've been here a while." The Black man's voice is a deep rumble. He points. "Skull there. Most of the ribs here. Pelvis. There's some vertebrae. I think we have a complete skeleton, it's just going to take us a while to gather it all up."

"Animals scattered them."

The Black man nods. "Do you see any personal effects? Clothing, stuff like that?"

The white man starts walking, his eyes on the ground. Then he stops and points. "There."

The Black man steps up next to him, then squats for a closer look. "Looks like…leggings, maybe? Oh, and here's a running shoe."

The white man steps around a crime scene tech and approaches the skull. "There's hair here, too. Looks to be brown. Long. Curly. In a ponytail." Now he looks a little sick.

"So likely a female, then."

The white man stares off into the distance for a while, fully zoned out. I wonder what he's thinking about.

The Black man watches him anxiously. "Mike."

Mike startles and clears his throat. "Uh. Yeah. Sorry, E. I'm– I'm back."

"Where did you go?"

Mike shakes his head irritably. "Nowhere."

E puts a hand on Mike's shoulder. "It's not your fault, Mike."

Mike frowns and his lower lip quivers ever so slightly. "I'm pretty sure it is, E." He takes a deep breath to steady himself.

E nods. "All right, let's focus. We've got a body to recover."

The men get to work, walking around the area with their eyes on the ground, looking for more evidence and marking it with little yellow plastic tents when they find it. The crime scene techs meticulously photograph, excavate, and document every one of my bones, along with my clothing and my charm bracelet. Mike spends extra time with the bracelet, turning it over and over in his gloved hands and examining it closely. "Cardinals appear when angels are near," he whispers. Nobody hears him but me. Then he carefully places the bracelet in a paper evidence bag and seals it shut.

I watch as they work, and glean a few interesting nuggets of information from their conversation.

Mike is Detective Mike Franklin. He's brand-new to the Investigations unit, fresh from patrol, and this is his first case as a detective. "E" is Eric Plummer. He's been a detective for seven years and is helping to train Mike.

Mike is a pretty good-looking guy, actually. He has a kind face, with sky-blue eyes that sit under a strong brow. His brown hair is cropped close to his head. His teeth are strong and even. But he looks…sad. Tired. The skin around his eyes is so dark it almost looks bruised. His broad shoulders roll forward a bit, like he's carrying some heavy weight that nobody can see.

He looks almost…haunted.

Recovery work eventually wraps up and the crime scene techs start loading my remains into a body bag. The rest of the evidence is carefully bagged and tagged. The men carry the body bag between them and the women have their kits and evidence bags as we make our way out of the forest.

That's right. I get to go too. I trail along behind and above them. Finally! Although I'm sad to leave my new cardinal friends. *Goodbye, Bella and Edward. Take good care of those babies.*

The walk to the edge of the forest is long, made more difficult by thick brush and rough terrain. Finally a parking lot opens in front of us, with a patrol SUV marked CITY OF SUPERIOR POLICE and a larger SUV marked WISCONSIN DEPARTMENT OF JUSTICE CRIME SCENE RESPONSE parked right along the edge closest to the woods. Is that where the mysterious person in the dark t-shirt parked when they came here to dump my body?

The body bag and evidence bags are loaded into the crime scene vehicle, and I realize I'm not going with the detectives. I'm super sad when the patrol car drives away; I feel drawn to the sad detective somehow. I feel like we need each other.

Instead the crime scene techs take me in the opposite direction. Maybe now would be a good time to go back to sleep. Whatever they're going to do with what's left of my body, I don't need to be awake for it.

∞

"Here you go, Mike." The woman's voice, loud and clear, wakes me up. "Now remember, it's highly unusual to allow evidence to be kept anywhere other than in my room. Chief says the chances of this case ever making it to trial are slim to none, so you can keep this at your desk – but it has to stay in this case."

"Yep, got it." I know that voice. I shift my view outward and am shocked and thrilled to see Mike Franklin. I don't know how long we were separated, but he looks exactly the same. He gratefully takes my charm bracelet, encased in a clear acrylic box, from Stella Durbin, the evidence tech. "Thank you."

Stella smiles. "You're welcome."

That's when I realize: the bracelet. I'm somehow tethered to the cardinal charm bracelet that was found with my remains. When it moves, I move. When it doesn't, I don't. Does this happen to other dead people, or am I a special case?

I follow along behind Mike as he navigates hallways and pushes through a door marked INVESTIGATIONS. This is a large windowless room with six desks lined up in two rows like a classroom. There's one office (the name plate on the door says R. NICHOLS), one conference room, at least a dozen filing cabinets lining the walls, and one industrial-sized coffee maker on a stained table in a corner. All but one of the desks is occupied; the empty desk appears to be a dumping ground for takeout menus, bent paper clips, and broken staplers.

"You finally found your way to the bullpen all by yourself, eh Mike?" An older detective with a bushy gray mustache and fat arms calls from the other side of the room.

"Yeah, fuck you too, Pete." Mike is smiling as he sits at his desk and carefully places the bracelet next to a framed photo of a smiling young woman holding an adorable toddler in a cute pink dress. Then he pulls a fresh manila folder out of one drawer and a black permanent marker out of another and writes CARDINAL

DOE along with a case number on the folder. He slips a few pieces of paper inside, then sits back and admires his very first case file.

This is where my journey with Mike Franklin begins.

PART 1:
THE SAD DETECTIVE

2024

CHAPTER 1

If you asked me how long I've been with Mike Franklin, I couldn't tell you exactly. I just know it's been a long time. We've been through a lot together. Watching him and his team work through hundreds of felony cases has been noisy and sometimes chaotic, but highly satisfying. Their close rate is impressive, too; they've managed to bring all of those cases to a resolution.

Well…all except one. Mine.

Mike usually arrives at work before the sun rises and leaves after the sun sets, so the only way I know it's a new day is when he walks into his office and turns on the light. And here he is, middle-aged now but still handsome, dressed in his usual khaki pants and black Superior Police polo shirt, his badge and his holstered gun hanging on his belt. His hair is more gray than brown these days, the lines across his forehead and around his mouth are deeper, and he has to wear glasses when he's reading reports or working on his computer. He shrugs his black leather bag onto the floor, then sits.

His office is purely functional, its walls white and bare. His desk is L-shaped, and its surface is tidy; the only items on it besides his computer are the framed photo of a young woman holding a cute baby, a framed pencil sketch of a woman's face, a small clear acrylic case, and a black plastic cup full of ballpoint pens. The kind with the clicky plunger thing on top. A guest chair sits between the desk and the door.

As he does most mornings, Mike picks up the clear acrylic case first. Inside the case is the silver charm bracelet that was found with my remains. I know it belongs to me, but I don't know how or when I got it. That's one of the many memories that are trapped behind some wall of sheer, unbearable terror. It's not an actual wall, but that's the only word I can think of to describe the barrier that stands between me and my memories of my life and my death. I still haven't figured out a way to get past it, even after all this time.

Mike spends a moment examining the bracelet, and then he carefully sets it back in its rightful place next to the framed pencil sketch. It's impressively realistic, and features big dark eyes, a rather thin nose and symmetrical eyebrows. The artist drew the hair pulled back from the face, and a mass of curls is visible behind one shoulder. I guess it's supposed to be me. Mike had the composite sketch done not too long after I was found in an effort to put a face to my remains. I have no idea if that's my face. I definitely don't recognize it. Mike had such high hopes that the sketch would generate leads and jump-start his investigation.

It didn't.

Mike leans over and pulls something from his bag: a handheld digital recording device. I'm not surprised to see it; Mike often records himself talking when he's alone in his office. He's been doing it for almost as long as I've been with him. It's basically his way of keeping a journal.

When Mike records himself he usually talks about his dreams, and they're only about two things: his late wife and daughter, or Cardinal Doe. That's it.

This one turns out to be the former. Mike reaches for the framed photo of his beautiful wife Rachel and adorable baby daughter Kylie and gazes at it for a long time. They're young and beautiful and happy, all smiles, captured forever in a photo. Mike is older now, grayer, and every one of the deepening lines in his face tells a sad story. He's a haunted man. Has been for a long time.

He flips a switch on the recorder with this thumb and speaks. "Mike Franklin, checking in. Today's date is —" he glances at the huge military-style watch on his left wrist "— Monday the twenty-second of July, oh-five-thirty hours." He pauses, thinking, then: "Rachel, do you remember when we took Kylie to her first carnival? It wasn't too long before —" he stops, reconsiders, then starts again. "It was a lot of fun, wasn't it? Kylie got to ride the kiddie roller coaster and we all rode the Ferris wheel. We could see our house from the top, do you remember that? The lake was so pretty, and it seemed to go on forever like the ocean." He pauses, thinking. Then: "Kylie tried cotton candy for the first time. Is there anything more pure than the smile on a kid enjoying her first taste of spun sugar?" He chuckles softly. "That was a good day. Maybe the last good day." A sigh escapes him. "Last night I dreamt we were there, and we were a happy family. You were even smiling." His voice starts to shake on that last word. "You — ah, you kissed me, and you told me you loved me, and you said 'You worry too much, Mikey. Everything's going to be okay.'" Mike blinks hard to keep the tears at bay. "It broke my heart. Because I–ah, I can't remember the last time you actually did any of those things."

Mike's chin drops to his chest and he sits like that for a long time. Then he lifts the recorder to his mouth and says, "God, I miss you. I miss you both so fucking much." His thumb flicks the button to off and he tosses the recorder back in his bag.

The happy dreams always seem to hurt Mike the most.

CHAPTER 2

Once all that's done, Mike can get to work. And he does.

He turns to his computer, slips his glasses on, and spends some time catching up on emails as his team trickles in. Maggie Conover sticks her head in the open door and wishes him a good morning. Maggie looks like a minivan-driving soccer mom with her curly blonde hair twisted back and held in place with a claw clip, but looks can be deceiving. She is an excellent detective, especially skilled in interrogations. She hands Mike a paper coffee cup. "Have a good weekend, boss?"

Mike turns to look at her over his glasses as he gratefully accepts the coffee. "Thank you. It was all right, how was yours, Mags?"

She shrugs. "Two words: softball tournament."

"Ah. How did they do?"

"They took second. Missed the chip by one run. Sofia took a cleat to the face at third during the championship game, so that's been some drama. She's lucky she didn't need stitches, but she's more concerned about the bruising and scabbing. She won't leave the house, says everyone will make fun of her."

"But did she get the out?"

Maggie grins. "Goddamn straight she got the out."

"Atta girl."

Maggie wishes Mike a good day and disappears. Mike sips his coffee as he types up a few more emails. Then he stands, walks to his office door, and bellows, "Morris! Let's go!" His voice is deep and loud and easily carries across the bullpen.

"Coming, boss." The disembodied voice, not quite as deep as Mike's, starts out faint but gets louder as its owner approaches Mike. "I was just logging into my computer."

Mike stands to the side and waves Dominic Morris through the door. Dominic (he goes by Nic) is the department's newest detective and a total snack. I don't know ages, but if I had to guess I'd say he's around thirty. He's almost painfully good-looking with his cropped and textured dark blond hair, enormous blue eyes, and straight white teeth. His own khaki pants and black polo look like they were made for his fit and trim body. And he's almost as tall as Mike, too.

I could literally look at him all day.

Nic came to Superior from the Duluth Police Department, replacing Pete Mumford, who recently retired. Nic just finished his stint at the police academy and has been integrating with the team to start field work. Maggie Conover is his "onboarding partner" for the rest of his probationary period.

The men sit in chairs on either side of Mike's desk. "How are you settling in?" Mike asks. "Is Conover getting you everything you need?"

"Yeah, she's cool. She looks great for her age, and somehow she keeps up with the rest of the team. I'm impressed."

Mike's eyebrows draw together in a disapproving frown.

Nic keeps talking, oblivious. "I had no idea Superior would be so different from Duluth."

Mike decides to let Nic's comment slide. "Smaller department, fewer resources, I imagine."

"That's exactly it." Nic leans back in his chair, then lifts a foot and rests it on the other knee. "I like it, though. In Duluth they're all about staying in your lane, don't mess with the status quo." He emphasizes those last words by using his fingers to make air quotes. "Hierarchy, you know? Here I'm getting the impression that I'll be able to roll up my sleeves and dig in more. Which is cool, because I don't mind getting my hands dirty."

"I'm glad to hear you say that." Mike turns his chair and retrieves a well-worn file folder from a desk drawer. I know this folder. It's still marked with CARDINAL DOE and the case number in black marker, only now it's battered and coffee-stained. That folder stays locked away in that drawer and never comes out – unless Mike has found someone special to share it with. "Because I have a case that I'd like you to take a look at."

Nic's eyes light up. "Yeah?"

"Yep, and it's so cold you could ice skate on it. Every new detective who joins my team gets a chance to crack it. All have failed so far."

Nic, who is staring at the file almost greedily, looks up. "I like a challenge."

Mike flips the folder open to reveal dog-eared and wrinkled pages inside. Sitting on top of those pages is a copy of the Cardinal Doe composite sketch.

"I'd like to introduce you to Cardinal Doe."

Nic sits up and slides his chair closer.

"Cardinal Doe is Superior's only unidentified person. Her remains were found in the Superior Municipal Forest on April 21, 2009. She was so deep in those woods that she might never have been found if it weren't for a determined German Shepherd called Sarge."

Nic takes the file from Mike and quickly pages through it. "Oh boy."

"Sarge's owner, an economics professor at UW-Superior named Jonathan Weiss, said Sarge disappeared for a few minutes while out for a walk and came back carrying what turned out to be a femur. He couldn't get Sarge to drop it. In fact, the dog was still holding the bone in his mouth when Austin Bane got there ten minutes later. He was a patrol officer back then. Have you met Austin yet?"

Nic shakes his head. "Not yet. I think I have a meeting with him later this week."

"Good," Mike says. "You'll want to talk to him about Cardinal Doe. He was the first on scene after the call came in."

"Got it."

"I was the detective on call, a noob like you, and I got the assignment." Mike's eyes glaze over and he doesn't say anything for a long time. I know he's caught in some pretty gnarly memories.

"You okay, boss?"

Mike blinks and clears his throat. His voice is gruff. "Fine. Fine. This, ah, this case is…well, let's just say it's important to me. Any detective will tell you that cases can sometimes change your life. And they all have a case that never leaves them." Mike gently lays a hand on the sketch of Cardinal Doe's face. "This is mine. It's my albatross. And I want to see it solved."

Nic nods solemnly. "I understand."

"The medical examiner determined that the body was that of a white female, aged approximately eighteen to twenty-four years. He estimated she'd been dead six months to a year."

"Cause of death?" Nic asks.

Mike shakes his head. "Couldn't be determined. She was a skeleton by the time Sarge retrieved her right thighbone."

Nic nods slowly, absorbing this.

Mike recites the case details from memory. "She had shoulder-length curly brown hair pulled back in a ponytail. She was wearing black leggings, no underwear, a white tank top and sports bra, and a pair of silver and blue running shoes."

"Sounds like a woman out for a jog," Nic says, still skimming the papers in the case file.

"That's my thought as well. She was wearing a silver charm bracelet on her right arm." Mike turns in his chair again and grabs the acrylic case, then turns back and hands it to Nic. "This is it."

Nic sets the file aside, takes the case from Mike, and examines the bracelet closely. "One of the charms has a cardinal engraved on it," he observes. "Is that why you call her Cardinal Doe instead of just Jane Doe?"

Mike nods. "It's the only truly unique thing we have of hers."

Nic goes back to the bracelet. "Angels appear when cardinals are near," he murmurs. He shakes the case gently, trying to change its position so he can see the other charms. "I'll be with you forever. Love, Mar," he reads. "Huh." He stares at the bracelet, his forehead crinkled. "This is really personal, boss. It's something somebody had made for a close friend or family member."

Nic's right. I don't know who "Mar" is, but they must have been somebody close to me. Why else would they have a charm bracelet engraved with a special message just for me?

God, I wish I could *remember*.

"You weren't able to chase this bracelet down?" Nic asks.

Mike shakes his head. "Nope. And believe me when I tell you I visited or called every jewelry store in a fifty-mile radius."

"Did you look online?"

"I did. Nothing."

Nic hands the bracelet back to Mike, who carefully sets it in its place. "Why do you keep this on your desk? Shouldn't it be in evidence?"

Mike's defenses go up a little bit. "Like I said, this case is very important to me. I made a promise to myself and to the victim that I would give her back her name, and I wanted to have something that would help me to not lose sight of that. After it was processed for evidence, Chief said I could keep it in my office as long as it stays in that case."

Nic opens his mouth as if to ask another question, then closes it. An internal battle plays out behind those gorgeous blue eyes. He wants to ask Mike why the Cardinal Doe case is so important to him, but isn't sure if it's his place to ask such a question.

I know why the case is so deeply personal for Mike. I've been here since the beginning.

When I first came to know him, Mike was a rookie detective, fresh from Patrol like Nic. He'd lost his wife and young daughter some time before that. He was in a pretty dark place, and as he worked the Cardinal Doe case he became more and more obsessed. It was like he came to see me, an unidentified dead girl, as his salvation. *I just gotta give her her name back. Then I'll be okay. I know it.* He whispered this once during a long night spent searching the internet for the source of the charm bracelet.

But the Cardinal Doe case went cold, and it almost destroyed him.

Nic decides not to go there, and I'm glad. Instead he asks, "What else did you drum up in your investigation?"

"We sent her clothing and jewelry to the DOJ crime lab in Wausau for testing and analysis. They found a spot of blood on the front of her shirt, extracted male DNA from it, and ran it through CODIS. No hits. No ID, no suspect."

"Any fingerprints? On the bracelet, maybe?"

Mike shakes his head. "No fingerprints, either. Skin cells on the bracelet are from the victim." He sighs. "I worked with a forensic anthropologist and the best sketch artist this side of the Mississippi to create a facial reconstruction based on her skull. Turns out a sketch isn't all that useful without a timeline. And I'm sure you know, it's damn near impossible to build a timeline without an ID."

"Sounds like a no-win situation," Nic says.

"It was. It is. I checked missing persons reports within a one hundred mile radius as well, in Wisconsin, Minnesota, even parts of Michigan's Upper Peninsula and southern Ontario. Found two that seemed promising at first, but I eliminated them pretty quickly."

I remember. Mike was almost giddy with the idea that one of the missing girls could be Cardinal Doe.

∞

"Holy shit," Mike breathes. It's really late; the bullpen is dark and silent, and the only light in the room is his computer screen. It casts a cold, bluish glow, painting his face in shifting tones of light and shadow. His eyes are wide and bloodshot. "Holy shit. I might've found her."

He grabs the nearest pen and scrawls two names on a random piece of paper: Joan Parton and Taylor Breastie. At least, that's my best guess. His handwriting is as bad as any doctor's. Maybe worse.

Mike throws the pen down and returns his attention to his computer. The printer next to Captain Nichols' office door whirs to life and spits out several sheets of paper. Mike grabs them and returns to his desk. He pores over the first report, reading aloud in a low voice.

"Let's see, first up we have Jo Ann Payton, a thirty-year-old mother of two who disappeared in the middle of her late night shift at the local gas station and convenience store in, ah, March of 2008."

I mean, I was pretty close with Joan Parton.

"Hm. Timing's about right, but thirty seems a little old." He flips to another page, and there's Jo Ann Payton's driver's license photo. Her limp, shoulder-length hair is blonde, and her roots are black. A bleach-and-box job if I ever saw one. Her lips have the distinct turned-in appearance of someone who is missing more than just a couple of teeth.

"Fuck," Mike moans. "No way that's her."

It's true. My hair was a gorgeous shade of chestnut brown, long and curly. And every single tooth was still in my skull when Sarge the German shepherd stole my leg bone.

Frustrated, Mike crumples the Jo Ann Payton report into a ball and tosses it in his garbage can. Then he sighs. "This is it. It's gotta be. Taylor Bresette, age eighteen. That's within the age range the M.E. gave me. I like that. Ah, she was last seen at her grandmother's house in Duluth in

November 2007." Mike ponders this for a second, then counts on his fingers. "Seventeen months. M.E. thinks my Doe has been dead more like six to twelve." His shoulders slump a little as he flips to the next page and examines the photo of a Native girl with smooth brown skin, long black hair, stunning almond-shaped eyes, and a strong, straight nose. Her expression is serious, her eyes cloaked in mystery.

"Hair is not curly," Mike observes. Something else in the report catches his attention. "What the — a congenital cervical rib? What the fuck is that?" He turns to his computer and searches. "An extra bone in the neck, present at birth." He groans and rifles through the files on his desk until he finds the Cardinal Doe autopsy report. "Son of a bitch." His teeth are clenched tight. He pushes the file away and sits back in his chair. Disappointment radiates from him like heat from a fire. He sits and stews for a few moments, then grabs his bag and digs out something silver. It looks like—

Oh wow, it's a flask. He unscrews the top and knocks back a healthy gulp. And then another one. Doesn't he realize he's still at work? At the freaking police station? Not only that, but it's super late and he still needs to drive home.

I guess none of that has occurred to him because he keeps gulping until the flask is empty. Then he gathers up his stuff and leaves.

Dear god, I hope he makes it home.

∞

I didn't realize it then, but that night was the beginning of a rapid downward spiral for Mike. His two leads not panning out was only the first of many disappointments in this case, and he didn't handle any of them well.

"What about the media?" Nic asks. "Did they help generate any leads?"

"We got coverage when she was found, and again when we released the facial reconstruction. No tips came in."

Nic blinks slowly. "Aggravating."

"No shit," Mike says. "I couldn't develop a single lead. Cardinal Doe went cold pretty quick after that."

And Mike's entire life unraveled.

"Where is Cardinal Doe now?" Nic asks.

"Nemadji Cemetery. I took up a collection and raised enough money to bury her in a nice plot under a pretty sugar maple tree. It turns bright red every fall." Mike's voice is wistful and heavy with regret. "It keeps growing while she's still nameless. Seems unjust somehow."

"I'm sorry you couldn't ID her, boss." Nic's forehead is crinkled again. "It sounds like you did everything right."

"I tried," Mike says. "And six other detectives have tried over the last fifteen years. Yet Superior's only Doe remains unidentified." Mike folds his hands on the desk in front of him. "I'd like you to take a crack at it."

Nic grins. "I already have ideas. I saw some cool stuff in Duluth that I think might help with this case. Let me read through the file and come back to you with a proposal."

"Is a week long enough for you?"

Nic nods. "Plenty."

"All right, I'll see you back here in a week. And let's plan to meet every week at least to talk about your progress. This case is your only priority."

Nic stands, gathers up the Cardinal Doe folder, and heads back out to the bullpen. There goes my eye candy.

Mike breathes deeply and rubs his face with his hands, then retrieves his recorder from his bag. "Mike Franklin, back again. I just wrapped up a meeting with my newest detective. Dominic Morris, or Nic as he prefers to be called, came to us just about a month ago from Duluth PD. A hungrier young man I've never seen. This kid wants to be a detective something fierce. Duluth wouldn't take a chance on him because he had two letters of reprimand for pretty minor infractions." He chuckles humorlessly. "Their loss is my gain. I believe he's got the cajones for the job. Might just need some coaching, because he's a cocky little fucker."

Mike pauses for a second, thinking, and then resumes. "Anyway, I officially put him on your case today." Now he's speaking directly to Cardinal Doe. "It remains to be seen if the cocky new detective with something to prove can find the answers that six competent detectives haven't in fifteen years. Well…I guess I wouldn't call myself competent. I had way too much baggage to ever do right by you."

By "baggage," he means the trauma of his wife's and daughter's deaths. What happened to them is a mystery I haven't been able to solve in all my time with Mike. He doesn't talk about it. Ever.

He sighs deeply and slips the recorder back in his bag. Then he turns his attention to his computer. Criminals never take a day off, and neither does the man tasked with catching them.

There's always work to do.

CHAPTER 3

Mike's days are typically filled with meetings. So many meetings. He regularly meets with Chief of Police Paul Schmidt, Captain Alexandra Reeves, who is his peer in the patrol unit, and Douglas County District Attorney Hart Macallan. His relationship with the press in Superior is less than stellar, but still, he handles press conferences and often interfaces with reporters so his team can focus on their important work.

On top of all that, his detectives are in and out of his office constantly to talk about their cases. Mike has five detectives on his team, and they handle all types of felonies: homicides, assaults, sex crimes, white collar crimes, property crimes, you name it. Eric Plummer is the stoic Black man who helped Mike recover my remains and work the scene. Simon Griffith is the team's unofficial tech expert and only about half in the closet. Maggie Conover has been around longer than anyone and is often referred to as the "team mom." Most recently, ambitious young gun Dominic Morris came across the St. Louis River to replace the recently-retired Pete Mumford. And then there's Jewel Roy. She's what I would want to be when I grow up, if that were an option for me. She started in patrol and came over to Investigations after Mike was promoted to Captain. She's the complete package, really: gorgeous, strong, takes zero shit from anybody, and generally is a badass. She wears that black SUPERIOR POLICE polo shirt like it's made for her, tucked into a tasteful pair of chinos. A simple black belt holds her badge and her holster. Her caramel-colored hair is just long enough to pull back into a smart-looking ponytail at the nape of her slender neck.

I don't know if Nic has noticed her yet, but he'd be blind if he didn't. I hope he's blind.

Mike recently told Chief Schmidt that he's finally got his lean and mean dream team. Even if none of them so far have been able to crack the Cardinal Doe case. The Chief suggested that maybe Nic will change that. Mike gave a skeptical little smile and said we'll see.

Sometimes I think, deep down, Mike really doesn't want one of his detectives to solve Cardinal Doe. He believes he should be the one to give me back my name, and he's never forgiven himself for failing to do that. The day he realized his case was cold was a tough one.

∞

Mike is alone in the bullpen, punching numbers on his desk phone to make a call. He looks awful. His face is pale and drawn and unshaven. Dark circles bruise the skin around his eyes, hollowing out his gaze. It's obvious he's been drinking too much and not sleeping enough. The composite sketch of Cardinal Doe lays next to his elbow on the desk.

He switches to the speakerphone just as the call is answered by a high-pitched, sing-songy voice. "Kristina Baldwin." Kristina is the crime reporter for local television station KBJR Channel 6. She and Mike have a decent working relationship, as far as I can tell. Sometimes I suspect she might be interested in more, but the feeling is not mutual.

"Hey. Kristina. It's Mike."

"I'm sorry, Mike who?"

Mike sighs. "Really? What's your problem?"

"Oh, so you're going to just pretend you didn't hang up on me last time we talked?"

He presses his lips together until they're almost invisible. "I've been very clear with you that my wife and daughter are off limits. Yet you started asking questions anyway. I don't know what else you expected."

"I report the stories that the people want, Mike. What Rachel did is one of the biggest stories this town has seen in years. People still ask about it, and we'd love to be able to give them an update."

Mike takes a deep breath in an effort to calm himself. "Rachel and Kylie are not a fucking story, Kristina."

Kristina, clearly put out, gives an exaggerated sigh. "Why are you calling, then?"

"I need your help."

"Of course you do."

"I need you to do another story on Cardinal Doe. Get this sketch out there again."

"Mike —"

"Please, Kristina. I don't have any other options. The Chief is going to put her case on ice and move me to something else if I don't start developing some leads." Mike's voice quivers ever so slightly. "Please. I'm desperate. I need to give this girl her name back." A single tear leaves a wet trail as it slides down his grizzled cheek.

Kristina's tone shifts to something a little closer to empathy. "I get it, Mike. I do. And I want to help. But there's no way Parker's going to greenlight it if you don't have anything new. Something more than just the sketch."

Mike closes his eyes and pinches the bridge of his nose. "Fucking Parker."

"He's the news director, Mike. My hands are tied. I'm sorry."

Mike's head starts doing something funky, like a hybrid of a nod and a shake. He's losing his cool, and fast. "All right, you know what, Kristina? You don't want to help me? Fine." He stands and leans over until his lips nearly touch the microphone in the phone's base. "Fuck you, Kristina. And fuck Parker, too. Nothing but fucking leeches, all of you." Mike hits the button to cut the line, but not before Kristina's voice squawks his name again. The shock and alarm are clear in her voice.

Then Mike picks the entire phone apparatus up, yanks the cords out of the back, and launches it against the wall with all of his strength. It shatters into several pieces and falls to the floor. He sweeps everything off his desk with one giant motion. Papers and pens and folders and photo frames land on the floor with a crash. Then he grabs his keys and storms out.

Maggie Conover is the one to discover the mess Mike left in the bullpen. It doesn't take her long to deduce what happened. She goes to get Chief Schmidt, who surveys the damage and heaves a huge sigh through his bushy walrus mustache. He's a big man in stature, with an even bigger heart. "He can't do this anymore, can he?"

Maggie shakes her head sadly. "No."

Chief Schmidt nods. "All right, then. I'm going to make some calls. You let me know immediately when he comes back."

"Yes, sir." Maggie goes about picking stuff up off the floor and setting it on Mike's desk as neatly as she can.

Mike finally does come back the next morning. He's late, and he's rumpled. I realize with mild horror that he's piss drunk and still wearing yesterday's clothes. My god, he's a mess. Where did he go last night to end up in this condition? And did he drive here like this?

Mike doesn't walk so much as stumble across the bullpen to his desk, and he almost misses his chair when he tries to sit. He picks up the bracelet in its case and just sits there, hunched over his desk, staring at it.

Maggie is the only other detective in the bullpen, and she watches all this with wide eyes, then goes to get Chief Schmidt. When he walks into the pen, his face, usually kind, is beet red with anger. "Mike."

Mike lifts his head a bit at the sound of his name, but doesn't look around. He just goes back to staring at the bracelet.

The Chief grabs Mike's arm, and that wakes him up. "Wha–? Hey! What the hell? Get your ha–" He stops talking when he realizes who's manhandling him, and his eyes widen. "Chief, I…it's not–"

"In my office. Now."

Mike tries to stand and almost falls over. Chief Schmidt takes his arm again and guides him out of the bullpen. Maggie watches them leave, then shakes her head as she turns to her computer.

I expect that Mike will be back shortly, but he doesn't show. Where did he go?

I get my answer later in the day when Chief Schmidt calls a meeting in the bullpen. Everyone sits at their desks and watches the Chief with wide eyes while he explains the situation. "Mike Franklin is taking a three-month leave of absence to deal with some personal issues."

"Is he coming back?" Pete Mumford asks.

"His job will be waiting for him should he choose to come back. I know you've all seen him struggle the last few months. He needs to get himself right."

Everyone nods in agreement.

"Captain Nichols will be available to help with Mike's caseload when he's back from vacation next week. Except Cardinal Doe. That case goes straight to storage. E, can you handle that?"

Eric Plummer nods soberly. "Yes, sir."

"Thank you. My door's open if you need anything, all right?"

Everyone thanks the Chief and he leaves.

Eric gets to work gathering up Cardinal Doe case files and loading them into a box. The framed pencil sketch and the bracelet in its case go in there too. When Eric carries the box out of the bullpen and I go with him, I know it's time to sleep for a while.

I have no doubt Mike will come back. I just hope he'll come find me when he does.

∞

In spite of everything, no matter who ends up solving the Cardinal Doe case, I know Mike will never give up on it.

It's the only thing keeping this lonely and tortured man going.

CHAPTER 4

This day begins as most do: Mike walks in, sets his bag on his desk, spends a moment with the bracelet, and then settles in for his workday. He spends a few minutes responding to emails, and then there's a soft knock on the doorjamb.

Mike turns in his chair and waves Jewel Roy in. "Come on in. Have a seat."

"Morning, boss." Jewel sets her laptop on the desk in front of her and sits primly on the edge of the chair, spine straight, shoulders back. Her posture is so perfect, I often wonder if she was a dancer earlier in life. How would I know to make that connection? I have no idea. That information must be somewhere in the memories I can't access. Her hair is pulled back in one of her smart-looking ponytails.

"What do you got for me?"

Jewel pulls a wisp of hair away from her eyes and expertly tucks it behind her ear. "The Allie Bergstrom case is going to be the death of me, I think."

Jewel has been talking to Mike about this case a lot lately. Allie Bergstrom was a 19-year-old freshman at the College of St. Scholastica in Duluth who was killed when the BMW M4 convertible she was in lost control on the Superior side of the

Interstate 535 bridge – known as the Blatnik Bridge – and rolled. Both Allie and the car's other occupant, St. Scholastica junior Jamison Downey, were ejected from the vehicle. Allie died at the scene. Jamison was taken to St. Luke's Hospital in Duluth with severe injuries, but survived. Wisconsin State Patrol crash reconstructionists would later determine that the car was doing at least ninety miles per hour over the bridge, and when it swerved hard to avoid another car on the approach into downtown Superior, it flipped and rolled five times. The vehicle left a trail of debris almost a quarter of a mile long.

As soon as Jamison could speak he claimed Allie was driving, not him. Jewel is skeptical; the car was registered to Jamison's father, Delaney David Downey – who happens to be the CEO of one of Minnesota's largest publicly held companies. Medics noted that Jamison had a strong odor of alcohol about him, and his blood alcohol content was measured at .16, twice the legal limit for driving, two hours after the crash.

Jewel had crime scene techs collect evidence from the wrecked car's steering wheel, seats, and dashboard for testing and analysis. She finally got the results from the crime lab at the Wisconsin Department of Justice, known as the DOJ, and they're not what she expected.

"I don't get it, boss," Jewel says. "I have evidence that points to Jamison being the driver. For one, the driver's seat was pushed almost all the way back. Way too far for Allie, who was barely five-foot-two, to reach the pedals. Jamison Downey stands well over six feet. And – AND –" Jewel's slender, ringless fingers dance across the trackpad as she pulls up a photo, turns the laptop to face Mike, and points. "That is Jamison's driver's license lying in the driver's side footwell." She looks at Mike with wide hazel eyes. "How can the DNA say something different? I mean, Allie died almost instantly and Jamison was unconscious when patrol and EMS got to the scene. There is no way either of them got up and adjusted the damn driver's seat after the crash."

Mike makes a low *hm* sound. "That is odd. Do you have a hard copy of the DNA report?"

"No, but I can print it now for you." Jewel grabs the printout and hands it to Mike as she sits back down.

Mike slides his readers on and holds the paper up in front of his face as he skims it. He looks like a middle-aged college professor with the glasses perched on the end of his nose like that. "It says the DNA on the steering wheel is a mixture of Jamison's and Allie's. It's Jamison's car, so it makes sense that his DNA is on the wheel." He pauses, reading, then: "It says her DNA was on the gearshift too."

A perfect little vertical line forms between Jewel's eyebrows as she opens another document. "Emma's report says the only fingerprints on the gearshift and the steering wheel are Jamison's."

Emma Linton is the lead DOJ crime scene technician on the case.

Mike lowers his paper and takes off his glasses. "Well then. We have a discrepancy that needs to be resolved. Harvey's going to make his determination based on this report, and he'll call it an accidental death. Once that happens, we're out. So you need to get to Patsy before this report does."

Dr. Harvey Ferrell is Douglas County's medical examiner, and Patsy Finch is the M.E.'s investigator assigned to the case.

Jewel closes her laptop and stands. "Right. I'll go call her now." She starts to turn toward the door, then stops and looks back at Mike. "You don't think –"

"That David Downey might have something to do with this? The thought crossed my mind." Mike tosses his glasses on the desk. "He's worth something like four hundred and fifty million. It's not a stretch to think he might put some of that money to work protecting his son."

Jewel nods and moves toward the door. She finds it blocked by Nic, who is balancing his open laptop and the Cardinal Doe case file in his arms. A giant grin spreads across his face when he sees Jewel. "Hey, sexy," he says.

Jewel rolls her eyes. "Fuck off, Nic." She pushes past him and out the door.

"Hey, I'm still waiting for that coffee I asked for," he calls after her. "Remember, one sugar, two cream." He looks at Mike, still grinning. The lines in Mike's forehead deepen in an epic frown.

My boyfriend is turning out to be kind of a douchebag. And he's about to be schooled in a most spectacular way.

Mike points to the chair where Jewel had been sitting. "Sit. Now."

Nic's grin falters. "Uh. Okay." He sits, looking a bit confused.

"I don't know how they do things in Duluth, but this department is not some boys' club and behavior like that will not be tolerated." Mike's sky-blue eyes simmer with anger.

Nic blinks. "It was just a joke, boss."

"Jokes are supposed to be funny. Jewel is a valued member of this team and she will be treated as such. Am I making myself perfectly clear?"

Nic maintains eye contact with Mike. Wow, he really is arrogant. "Perfectly."

"You're not getting off to a spectacular start here, Nic," Mike says. "I suggest you do a little soul-searching about your opinion of yourself and how you treat others if you want to stay here."

Nic's eyes finally fall and he studies his hands. "Sorry, boss."

"Don't apologize to me, apologize to her." Mike nods toward the door. Jewel is leaning against the door frame, arms crossed, chin up, eyebrows raised.

Nic's face turns pink and he stammers. "Look, Jewel, I –"

"Apology accepted." She disappears.

Mike sighs. "All right. What do you have for me?"

Nic rearranges his things, sliding the case file to the side and setting the laptop on the desk. Then he turns it so Mike can see the screen. "I have forensic genetic genealogy."

Mike squints and leans closer, then slides his glasses back on. "All the rage these days," he mutters.

"Damn straight," Nic says. "It's helped solve over six hundred cold cases in the last few years. Can you believe that? Cases that were decades old and so cold you could ice skate on them, just like Cardinal Doe. Cases that they thought would never be solved."

Mike leans closer to Nic's laptop and blinks, intrigued. I can't quite tell what's on the screen. A presentation slide, maybe? Or a website?

"You said you have DNA," Nic reminds him.

Mike nods. "We do."

"Then we have what we need to do this."

"Huh." Mike rests his elbow on his desk and his chin in his hand, reading. "This sounds expensive, Nic."

"It is. Earlier this year Duluth used this technology for the first time on a thirty-five-year-old John Doe case. They exhumed his body and took tooth pulp, then sent it to a private lab based in St. Paul called ForenTech. The lab ran the DNA, then uploaded the profile to one of those genealogy databases and found some distant familial matches. They used that information to build a family tree and eventually located a first cousin in St. Cloud, Minnesota. That led to an ID."

Fascinated, Mike says, "I think I remember that case. The John Doe was found dead inside a railroad shed in the dead of winter, right?"

Nic nods. "Right. The victim turned out to be a thirty-year-old man named Robert Martin. His family hadn't seen him since August of 1988, and his body was found in late January of 1989. His blood alcohol was through the roof. They figure he was homeless and intoxicated and tried to hide from the cold in this little metal shed at the Rice's Point railyard. He ended up freezing to death and nobody knew his name for thirty-five years."

"But he got his name back," Mike says softly.

"Eventually, yeah."

"How much did Duluth pay for ForenTech's services?"

"I called Jake Dillon, the detective who handled the case, and asked. He said it was about fifteen grand, all in."

Mike gives a low whistle and removes his glasses. "Well, I know I don't have that kind of money in my budget. How do you propose we pay for this little adventure?"

"Crowdfunding," Nic says.

Mike leans back in his chair as realization dawns on his face. "Ah." He runs a hand over his lips and chin as he thinks. "We can't accept donations directly as a matter of policy, but the department's community outreach program might be able to help. They could collect on our behalf. Check with Andrea Pining over there." He pronounces the first name *AWN-dreea*. "Send her to me if she has any questions."

Nic spins his computer back to face him and starts typing. Then he says, "I have the head honcho's contact info, I can call down to ForenTech and get an estimate. Maybe set up a call to discuss."

Mike picks up a pen and starts clicking it fast with his thumb. Is he nervous? Excited? I can't tell. Maybe both. "I raised money the old-fashioned way back in '09 for Cardinal Doe's burial. The people here in Superior are generous. You'll get the money, I have no doubt."

"Thanks, boss." Nic closes his computer. "I'm excited to get started."

Mike tosses the pen back on his desk. "Good. Now get out of here and go make shit happen. And close the door behind you."

Nic gathers up his things and leaves. Mike sits and stares at the wall for a little while, then fishes his recorder out of his bag and starts talking.

"Mike Franklin, checking in. Today's date is Monday the twenty-ninth of July, oh-nine-forty hours. Nic proposed an idea for moving your case along." He's talking to Cardinal Doe. "And frankly, it's an excellent idea. One that really could be a game-changer." He pauses, thinking. "Forensic genetic genealogy." Another pause. "I've read about it. And yet it never occurred to me to look into it for your case." He closes his left hand into a fist and hits his desk with it, hard enough to make things rattle a little. "Am I losing my edge?"

Mike is interrupted by a knock on his door. He stops recording and sets the device aside. "Yeah. Come on in."

Eric Plummer opens the door partway and sticks his head in. He has a face like a basset hound and his kinky hair is more salt than pepper these days. "You okay, boss?"

Mike waves him in. "I'm fine."

Eric comes all the way into the office. He's more gangly than muscular now, and he walks slightly stooped over because his back always hurts him. He limps a little, too. Something about a degenerative disease of the discs in his lower spinal column. He likes to joke that his days of chasing suspects and wrestling them to the ground are over. Now he leaves that to the young cops and catches the bad guys from his desk. "I heard talking through the door." He takes his time sitting in the chair recently vacated by Nic, and he's holding a piece of paper.

"Remember when the Chief gave me the ultimatum to either go to treatment or lose my job?" Mike asks.

Eric nods. "When Cardinal Doe went cold."

"Right. While I was there, they taught us how to keep a journal. I did my best, but man…I never got the hang of writing in it. When I got back I decided to try recording myself talking instead of writing in a notebook. That did the trick for me, and

I've been doing it ever since. When I run out of space on my recorder, I just go buy a new one. I have no idea how to get my recordings off the damn things." He points across the room. "One of the drawers in that filing cabinet is full of recorders. And mini cassette tapes from back before everything went digital."

Eric chuckles. "We've been together a long time, and just when I think I know everything about you, you drop something new on me."

"I'm an enigma," Mike says. "What do you got for me, E?"

Eric's entire demeanor sobers. "I got a concern, boss."

"Lay it on me."

Eric hands him the paper he brought in with him. "Read this email."

Mike puts his glasses back on as he takes the paper from Eric. He reads it, and deflates a bit. "Goddammit, Nic," he mutters.

"I'm a 'credit to my race'," Eric says bitterly. "As if he was surprised such a great idea could come from a Black man."

"I'm sorry, E," Mike says. The stormcloud is back over his brow. "I had to correct him earlier for making an asshole comment to Jewel, too. I will handle this. Thanks for letting me know."

Eric stands up gingerly, wincing, and shuffles to Mike's office door. "Thanks, boss." And he was gone.

Mike shakes his head and picks his recorder up again. He hits the button with his thumb, sighs deeply, and says, "Maybe Duluth was on to something. Nic's displaying overtly racist and misogynistic behavior. Note to self, ask Simon if Nic has said anything offensive to him." Another sigh escapes him. "I can't have him alienating anyone on my team. I hope I didn't make a big mistake." He turns the device off and tosses it into his bag, then turns his attention to his computer.

I hope that's all it is. Nic may be good-looking, but damn. The fact that he's a card-carrying bigot is a real turn-off.

Who needs a boyfriend like that?

CHAPTER 5

Mike calls Simon Griffith into his office first thing after saying his daily hello to my charm bracelet. Within seconds Simon is standing in the doorway. "You wanted to see me?"

"Yeah. Close the door and have a seat."

Simon does as he's told, an uncertain look on his chiseled face. Honestly, I think he should be a model instead of a cop. His green eyes could pierce armor and his mop of curly black hair is the stuff of legend. The team knows he's gay, but he's not overt about it while at work. His life outside work is a totally different story. So I hear.

"How are things going with Nic?" Mike asks.

Simon sighs and crosses his legs at the knees. "Nic is the type of guy to make underhanded comments, then play them off as a joke. Or, if you call him out on it, he tries to gaslight you, convince you he didn't actually say what you heard him say with your own ears. It's juvenile."

Mike presses his lips together. "Personal experience?"

Simon rolls his eyes. "Just yesterday he asked me when I knew I liked guys, and if I've ever been with a woman just to make sure. Like, what the hell? That's like me asking him how he knows he likes girls. I said, 'Are you serious?', and he just laughed and told me I need to learn to take a joke."

Mike sighs. "Thanks for the info, Simon. I'll take care of it."

"Need anything else?"

Mike shakes his head and Simon goes back to his desk. Mike spends a few minutes typing some notes on his computer until Nic appears at his door, laptop under one arm. "Ready for the call with ForenTech, boss?"

Mike glances at Nic over his glasses, then looks at his watch. "Yeah, come on in. What's her name again?"

"Michelle…something," Nic says as he sits. Mike arranges his computer so everyone can see each other. Mike clicks a few things with his mouse and a smiling face appears on the screen. She's pretty, probably in her mid to late forties, and her wavy shoulder-length hair is almost completely white. I've never seen hair like that before. It's gorgeous.

"It's nice to meet you both," she says after Mike and Nic introduce themselves. "My name is Michelle Musgrove, I am the founder and head of lab sciences at ForenTech. We're a premier forensic laboratory based in St. Paul, Minnesota."

"You come highly recommended by our colleagues in Duluth," Mike says. "You recently helped them solve a John Doe case from 1989."

Michelle nods. "That's right. The victim's name was…ah, it's escaping me at the moment." Her face takes on a pinkish hue as she struggles to remember.

"Having a bit of a senior moment there, Michelle?" Nic asks, grinning. He looks at Mike as if expecting him to agree. Or laugh. Or both.

Mike does none of those things. The look on his face suggests he'd like to take Nic out back and kick his ass. "Give us a second, okay Michelle? We'll be right back."

Michelle nods. Her face is unreadable.

Mike mutes his computer and turns off the camera, then looks at Nic with blazing eyes. "What the fuck was that?"

Nic's eyes widen and the shit-eating grin fades. "What do you mean?"

"A 'senior moment?' Are you fucking kidding me?"

"It was a joke, boss."

Mike's hands clench into fists, and for a brief second I think he might haul off and hit Nic. Instead he says, "Get out."

"What? Why?"

"Take the rest of the day off, Nic. Go home. I don't want to see your face until tomorrow."

Something on Mike's face convinces Nic not to push him any further. He stands, gathers his things, and leaves Mike's office without another word.

Mike takes a couple deep breaths to steady himself, then resumes the video call with Michelle Musgrove. "Hey, Michelle. Thanks for waiting. Sorry for the delay."

Michelle nods, her face still stoic.

"Look, I need to apologize for my detective's behavior. That comment was completely uncalled for."

"I wish I could say it was the first time I've heard a comment like that," Michelle says. "It happens all the time, unfortunately. If it's not my age, it's my gender. Sometimes it's both."

"That doesn't make it acceptable." Mike picks up a pen and clicks it rapidly with his thumb. "I expect my team to treat everyone with respect. I'm very sorry that didn't happen here, and I hope his behavior doesn't affect your decision to work with us on our case."

"Robert Martin." A small smile plays at Michelle's lips.

"I'm sorry?"

"The John Doe in Duluth. His name was Robert Martin."

Mike smiles back, relieved. "I have a fifteen-year-old Jane Doe case I'm hoping you can help with. We call her Cardinal Doe."

Michelle asks about the case and he fills her in on the details.

Echoing what Nic had said, Michelle says, "If you have DNA from your victim, then you have everything I would need to help with your case. How it works is typically we run a short tandem repeat test for autosomal DNA first, as that is the most comprehensive. I'll explain why. Do you have kids, Captain Franklin?"

Mike's face pales, and he looks down at his hands.

Michelle doesn't notice and keeps talking. "Autosomal DNA is inherited equally from both parents, so fifty percent of your child's DNA comes from you, the father, and the other fifty percent comes from the mother. No two people share the same autosomal DNA, except identical twins. That's what makes it so powerful. All of the major DNA testing companies also test autosomal DNA, which means there are millions of profiles in publicly available databases that we can compare to. Tens of millions."

I don't understand most of the big scientificky-sounding words Michelle is saying, but she said one word I do know: parents. I must have had parents when I was alive, although I don't remember them. Sometimes I imagine that my father was a handsome, strapping man who heroically saved people, maybe a police officer like Mike. My mother was a powerful corporate executive, the boss of hundreds or thousands of people. Maybe I had a brother or a sister, or both. And of course we had a dog. A big fluffy golden retriever named Bruno who liked to fetch up sticks.

I have to imagine because I don't know. Memories of my family, like all the others, are out of my reach. I don't know if I'll ever be able to make those memories mine again.

"What happens if you don't find a DNA match in those databases?" Mike asks, regaining his composure.

"That is highly unlikely. There are other DNA tools we can look at, but they would require additional samples you may not have, or be able to get. For example, we can test mitochondrial DNA for the maternal line or Y-chromosomal DNA for the paternal line, but there are no databases for those. You would need reference samples to compare to. And given that you have an unidentified Jane Doe – I'm sorry, Cardinal Doe – I assume you don't have those."

"Correct."

"Then we'll have to hope the autosomal DNA gives us what we need." Michelle says. "I believe it will."

Mike is clicking his pen super fast again. "Can you put together a proposal for us?"

"Absolutely."

"How long does this typically take?" Mike asks.

Michelle nods. "Once I receive payment and the samples, it will take about two weeks to run the tests and generate profiles. Then we'll upload the profiles to the OurDNA database. You may be familiar with it; it's the largest publicly accessible DNA database in the world."

Mike considers this, then says, "So you're saying there's a chance."

This makes Michelle smile. Her teeth are as white as her hair. "I won't know for sure until we dive in, but based on what I'm hearing I'd say there's a decent chance we'll be able to help give Cardinal Doe her name back."

"That's what I like to hear," Mike says, and grins. He hardly ever smiles, but when he does, it transforms his entire face. I love how his eyes crinkle at the corners. "I'll get those files over to you today."

"Sounds good. Once I have those, I should be able to put together a proposal in a day or two. Thank you."

"We'll be in touch." Mike ends the call, then props his elbows on his desk and lays his head in his hands. He sits like that for a long time, then turns to look at the photo of his wife and daughter. That's when I realize his cheeks are wet. Michelle asking him if he had kids must have really rattled him.

I wish I knew what happened to Rachel and Kylie. He never talks about it, but I've managed to pick up little clues over the years. One fiery phone conversation with Kristina Baldwin shortly before his breakdown was especially telling.

∞

"Here you go, Mike." Tierney Powell, SPD's community relations lead, lays a single printout at Mike's elbow.

Mike glances at it. "What is it?"

Tierney stands maybe five feet tall in athletic shoes and her gorgeous golden hair is cropped in an adorable shaggy bob. She handles external communications and public relations for the department. "It's the press release you requested. Just got it out on the wire."

"Oh!" Mike snatches it up and starts reading. "Sweet. Thanks, Tierney."

She smiles. "No problem. I'll let you know when we start getting calls."

Soon enough the first call comes in and is routed to Mike. He's alone in the bullpen so he answers on speakerphone. He prefers that over holding the phone's receiver so he can multitask. "Franklin."

"Hi Mike, it's Kristina Baldwin, KBJR." Her sing-songy voice is instantly recognizable.

"Hey, Kristina. How are you?"

"I was happy to see your press release. You have new information on your Jane Doe?"

"We call her Cardinal Doe. And yes, I have a new composite sketch," Mike says proudly. "I would love it if you could run a story tonight, get it in front of as many eyeballs as possible."

"I'll check with Parker, but I don't think it'll be a problem." Kristina's voice turns bright. "Mind if I ask you a couple additional questions?"

Mike frowns. "Everything you need is in the press release."

"No, I mean about something else. You have a big anniversary coming up, don't you?"

A full-on scowl settles on Mike's face. "What do you mean?"

"Aren't we just a couple weeks away from a year since Rachel and Kylie died?"

Mike's mouth drops open in complete shock. "Excuse me?"

"Well, I'm thinking, and Parker agrees, that we should do a five-minute feature on the anniversary of their deaths. I would interview you, you tell me and our viewers how you're coping and how your life has changed since your wife—"

"No." Mike's tone is flat as a board.

"Look, just hear me out, okay? I think the community—"

"I don't care what the community thinks. The answer is no."

She presses on, undeterred. "Why do you think Rachel would do something so drastic? Was it something you said or did, do you think?"

Mike closes his eyes and takes a deep breath. "Listen carefully, Kristina, because I'm only going to say this once. My family and my life are not for you to exploit for ratings, do you understand me? Rachel and Kylie are off limits. Back off."

Kristina's voice turns huffy. "Well, I don't know if I can air a Cardinal Doe story if you won't—"

"Then don't air it. I don't give a fuck. You're not the only game in town, Kristina. In fact, I've got Jack Mendoza from the Duluth News Tribune waiting for me on the other line." A little, but clearly necessary, white lie.

Kristina tries again. She really does have a set of stainless steel balls, doesn't she? "But Mike, the concerned public wants to know: why did Rachel do what she did? They deserve answers, and this is your chance to tell your story. Control the narrative. I think—"

Mike jabs the button and hangs up on her in mid-sentence. His fists are clenched and his breathing is shallow and fast. He squeezes his eyes shut and takes several deep breaths. Tears leak out from under his eyelashes. He takes a break from his breathing exercises long enough to mumble, "She did what she did because of me. It's my fault. Okay? Is that what you want to hear?" He resumes his deep breathing, slowly, finally getting himself under some semblance of control. His computer dings, and he pulls up the new email that just landed in his inbox. It's from Kristina.

`We'll run the Cardinal Doe story. Let me know if you change your mind about yours.`

"Yeah, right," Mike mutters and deletes the email.

∞

Whatever Rachel did, it traumatized Mike so badly that he can't bring himself to talk about it, even after all this time. He grieves as hard for them now as he did then. It's really hard to watch.

Eventually he puts the photo back, takes a deep breath, and wipes his face. It's time to get back to work.

No rest for the weary, I guess.

CHAPTER 6

Mike arrives earlier than usual this morning; the view through his window is still pitch black. The bullpen is dark and quiet too. He walks into his office like a man on a mission. Enormous, bruise-like circles frame his eyes. He looks like he didn't get a wink of sleep last night.

He closes the door and beelines to his desk. He pulls a drawer open and rummages almost frantically until he finds what he's looking for: his recorder. He accidentally left it there yesterday. He presses the button and paces as he talks.

"Mike Franklin, checking in. Ah, today is Monday, the fifth of August, oh-five-hundred hours. Last night I dreamed about Kylie." He's walking and talking so fast in this small space that he's a bit out of breath. He runs a hand over his close-cropped hair, then takes a ragged breath to try and steady himself. "The dream was exactly like that day. Every light in the house is on. I'm walking slowly up the stairs, calling for Rachel, calling for Kylie, and there's no response. I realize I can hear water dripping. Plink-plink-plink." He heaves in another breath without stopping his frantic pacing. "I start running, and when I reach the top landing, the bathroom is right there in front of me, and I see a little foot. A tiny little foot hooked over the edge of the bathtub."

He stops pacing and doubles over, his heavy breaths transforming into deep, agonized sobs. Then he stands up straight again and fights to gain control of himself. "I–ah, I fall to my knees next to the tub and there's my baby girl, floating facedown in the full bathtub." Another harsh sob. "She's dead. My baby's dead and all I can do is scream. But then – but then Kylie lifts her head and looks at me, her eyes black and full of water, and says, 'Why I dead, Daddy? Why I dead?'"

Mike falls to his knees as the sobs take over. He covers his face with his hands and lets them come. After they've finally run their course, Mike sits back against his desk, swipes one hand across his face, and realizes he's still holding the recorder in the other. "That's when I woke up. I didn't have the chance to tell her she's dead because her Mommy killed her." His voice cracks on that last word and fresh tears trickle down his grizzled cheeks.

If I had a heart, it would wail an anguished song like the howling wind. If I could cry, rain would fall like tears from a grieving sky. If I had arms, I would wrap Mike in healing warmth and protect him from his heartbreak. But I can only watch as he sits on the floor of his darkened office, broken and alone.

He finally speaks again. "Kylie would have turned seventeen this year. She should be in high school, doing all the things that teenagers do. Rachel and I should be cheering her on in her activities, helping her navigate boys and grades and looking at colleges." A deep sigh. "Rachel's monsters took it all away. And my life…just stopped." Mike leans his head back, closes his eyes, and lets the device fall from his hand. It lands on the carpeted floor with a quiet thud.

He sits like that for a long time. The sky outside his window goes from black to gray to pink to orange as the sun rises. What finally rouses him is the muffled sound of a voice outside his closed door. He stands up, stretches, and rubs his tired face with his hands. He picks the recorder up off the floor and sticks it in his bag where it belongs. Then he sits in his chair and starts his work day as if nothing happened.

I don't know how Mike can just set his emotions aside like that. It's easy to look at him and think he's doing fine and has his life together, when in reality he is barely hanging on.

I wish I could do something to help.

The station slowly comes to life outside Mike's door. Eventually he calls Nic into his office. Nic appears at the door. He's trying to project confidence, but the trepidation in his eyes betrays him.

"Have a seat."

Nic sits, and cowers just a little under the weight of Mike's angry gaze. I think he finally realizes he's in more than a little bit of trouble.

"About that asshole comment you made to Michelle Musgrove yesterday."

Nic tries to speak. "I–"

Mike holds up a hand. "Save it. I don't want to hear that it was just a joke. You fucking embarrassed me yesterday."

Nic holds Mike's gaze, but his ears are burning red. "I'm sorry."

"E stopped by the other day and showed me an email where you called him a 'credit to his race'." Mike tosses the printout in front of Nic.

Nic frowns as he scans it. "Well, yeah. He had an awesome idea for where to go to make a phone call that I don't need everyone to hear. I didn't know there was such a thing as a mother's room. He said nobody uses it and it's perfect for when you need a little privacy."

"And what, exactly, does his great idea have to do with his race?"

Nic's eyes widen as realization dawns on his face. "What? No. No no no, it was a compliment. I swear. I'm no racist. I don't see color."

Mike leans over his desk, propping himself on his elbows. "That was no compliment. Eric received it as a microaggression meant to make him feel somehow less than because he's Black. And then you make it ever so much worse with that stupid comment." Mike's eyes are on fire. "If you didn't 'see color' —" he emphasizes this with air quotes — "you would never have said something so stupid about his race."

Nic opens his mouth as if to argue, then closes it again. Smart choice.

"In the past few days, since you came over from the academy, you have managed to insult every one of your teammates and a potential partner. I'm beginning to see why Duluth wouldn't promote you. You're a fucking bigot."

Boom. I wish I could clap and cheer.

"But —"

Mike holds up a hand again. "You're a grown-ass man and I can't believe I have to say this out loud, but we do not speak that way to anyone, ever. You are expected to treat everyone with respect and dignity. And when I say everyone, I mean *everyone*, regardless of your beliefs or political persuasion. Teammates, superiors, partners, vendors, the press, the public, even suspects. Am I making myself clear?"

Nic drops his eyes and nods, finally chastened.

"Let me remind you that you are still on probation. I could let you go right now and not think a single thing of it." Mike leans back in his chair. "But I'm not going to do that. Against my better judgment, I'm going to take a page from the book of Paul Schmidt and give you one last chance because I believe you have excellent potential, Nic." I remember Chief Schmidt saying something very similar to Mike back when Mike was a new detective, struggling with the Cardinal Doe case.

"However. You're going to have to work your ass off to convince me that you're worth taking a chance on. If I can't trust you to behave appropriately with your team, how in the hell can I trust you to behave appropriately with the people you're supposed to protect and serve?"

"I understand. I'll do better."

"I hope so." Mike lets the uncomfortable silence draw out a bit before speaking again. "I need you to gather up the Cardinal Doe reports and get them to Michelle Musgrove. She's going to put together a proposal for us."

"Okay, boss." Nic leaves, his big ego a bit deflated. I hope his change in demeanor means Mike finally got through that thick skull.

If he leaves, who will be my eye candy?

CHAPTER 7

Mike is so completely engrossed in the report he's reading that a loud knock on his door makes him jump inches off his chair. "Come in," he bellows, the adrenaline jolt making his voice shake a bit.

Nic enters, his gorgeous blue eyes blazing. "We did it, boss."

"Jesus Christ, you scared the piss out of me." Mike's reading glasses are perched on the end of his nose. "What did we do?"

Nic goes to a chair and sits. "Whoa. Uh. Don't take this the wrong way, boss, but you don't look so hot. Are you feeling okay?"

Mike dismisses this with a wave. "I'm fine. What did we do?"

"We raised twenty thousand dollars for Cardinal Doe."

"Already?"

Nic grins. "We got it done in just over a week."

"Well, I'll be damned." Mike's voice, usually deep and confident, is strained and crackly. It isn't until he takes off his glasses and wipes his eyes with the back of his hand that I realize he's fighting back tears. "H-how?"

"Andrea and her community engagement team are magicians, man. They have an online crowdfunding account, a huge email list, and ten thousand social media followers. They ran a campaign to drive donations to the online fundraiser. They got local media coverage, too. One of the TV stations, I think it was KBJR, had their reporter do a quick story about it during the morning news last Thursday. I talked to her, her name's Kristina. She seems like a nice lady. She asked how you're doing."

Mike ignores this. "This is very impressive, Nic."

Nic chuckles. "She said you might pretend she doesn't exist. She asked me to keep her posted on the case."

"Yeah, so she can find a way to exploit a tragedy for ratings." Mike's voice is bitter.

"You weren't kidding when you said the Superior community is a generous one. Andrea said they've never hit a fundraising goal so quickly."

Mike nods, saying nothing, but I know what he's thinking: *They remember her.* Then he clears his throat and says, "Well then, I guess you'd better gather up everything Michelle Musgrove needs to run her tests and ship it off to her."

"Where would I find that?"

"The medical examiner's office has all of the biological specimens taken from Cardinal Doe at autopsy," Mike says. "I would start with Patsy Finch over there; if she can't help, she'll know who can. Clothing and other evidence are in storage. Stella Durbin is our evidence tech, she can help you track those down."

Nic slides a tattered notebook toward him from the edge of Mike's desk and flips through until he finds a blank page. Then he uses one of Mike's pens to jot both names down. "Got it."

"Start there, and if you need anything else just let me know." Mike slides his glasses back on his nose.

Nic tears the sheet out of the notebook and heads for the door.

"Nic?"

Nic stops and turns back. "Yeah?"

"Excellent work."

Nic's face turns pink. "Thanks, boss." He leaves.

Mike fishes his recorder from his bag and turns to look at the Cardinal Doe sketch. "Mike Franklin, checking in, August ninth, oh-nine-forty-five hours. Nic just came by to tell me he's raised more than enough money to retest the evidence in your case. Michelle's proposal said it would cost fifteen grand. Nic raised twenty. By god, this really could work." He pauses, thinking. Then: "I've spent countless hours over the years thinking about what your name might be. At one time I thought it was Jo Ann, or Taylor. Now I wonder if it's something like Courtney or Stephanie. Maybe Ashley." A longer pause. "Or Rachel." Mike's brow furrows and he glances at the photo of his family. "Am I right? Hopefully we'll know soon."

Mike puts the recorder away just as Eric Plummer appears at his door. "I got a conundrum on the Wallace case, boss."

"Come on in, E."

Eric sits in the chair Nic just vacated and takes in Mike's condition with some concern. "You all right, boss?"

"I've had better days, but I'll be fine. Before we talk about Dooley Wallace, our favorite white collar criminal, let me ask you a question."

"Shoot," Eric says. His deep voice rumbles in his throat.

"How are things going with Nic? Since you showed me that email?"

Eric blinks. "Oh, just fine. He apologized. Whatever you said to him really stuck, boss. He's a lot more conscious of the words that come out of his mouth. He's actually a pretty cool cat."

Mike nods slowly, absorbing this. "Is he treating Jewel better too?"

Eric shrugs. "Seems to be. Those two are getting along fine." He gives Mike a wink that I don't like. Not one bit.

A small chuckle escapes Mike. "Great. Just great. Might be time to give the team a refresher on our workplace conduct policies."

The men move on to talking about Dooley Wallace's latest escapades.

I'm worried about Mike. It's like the more progress Nic makes on the Cardinal Doe case, the more Mike seems to exhibit the same distressing behaviors that put him in treatment after the case went cold the first time. Nightmares, insomnia, emotional breakdowns – it's all a little too familiar. It's not a stretch to think he could start drinking again as a way to cope.

I hope Nic Morris can solve my case.

For Mike's sake.

CHAPTER 8

When Mike walks into his office, I know immediately that he had another nightmare last night. It's written all over his exhausted face. I watch as he pulls his recorder out of his desk drawer – he'd forgotten it again – and proves me right.

"I'm back in the Superior Municipal Forest." The recorder is sitting on his desk, between his elbows, and his head is in his hands. I can't see his face. His voice, an exhausted monotone, echoes off the wooden desktop. "I'm running, and it feels like the trees and brush are trying to stop me. They know what's in there." A pause. "But I keep pushing through. I know where I'm going because I've been here before. Fifteen years ago."

Mike pauses again, longer this time. His breathing is steady, so I know he's not breaking down. Yet. Then: "There it is. I see it now. It's just a glimpse of white from here, but it takes shape as I get closer to it. It's your skull." His breathing takes on a raggedy quality; he's struggling to contain his emotions. "It looks exactly as it did on the day you were found. Except…it's changing. It's morphing, becoming a face. But it's not your face. It's my wife's."

Mike's shoulders tremble and tiny puddles appear on the desk where his tears fall. "It's Rachel. Her eyes suddenly pop open and roll around in their sockets a few times before they land on me.

Those eyes are overflowing with white-hot hatred. Her mouth opens and the most awful sound comes out. It's like the metal-on-metal screech of bad brakes on a semi." Mike's voice hitches. "But still I hear her words. 'All your fault, Michael. ALL. YOUR. FAULT.'"

An extended silence, broken only by his hiccupy sobs. Then: "I woke up screaming."

Rachel's photo has been sitting on Mike's desk for as long as I've been around. I know what she looked like in life: petite, slender, long brown hair, enormous brown eyes that remind me of a fawn's. I couldn't imagine those baby deer eyes filled with white-hot hatred. She looked so gentle. And her daughter was her spitting image, save for one feature: Kylie had inherited her daddy's sky-blue eyes.

I wonder again what had happened and how it could possibly have been Mike's fault.

Mike finally lifts his head and turns off the recorder. His eyes are puffy, and the lines across his forehead seem a little deeper. He looks like life has become an intolerable burden instead of something wondrous to be experienced. I want to tell him that Nic is going to solve the Cardinal Doe case and lift that responsibility from his shoulders, if he can just hang on. The case won't let Mike go so he can heal. I know now that I am what holds him back.

I always have been.

Mike moves slowly, and it takes him a little longer, but he gets himself put back together enough to tackle his work. Just in time, too; Nic soon appears in Mike's office for another video call with

Michelle Musgrove. If he notices Mike's bedraggled appearance, he doesn't let on.

When Michelle's face appears on Mike's computer screen, Nic speaks before anybody else can. "Michelle, I owe you an apology. What I said was insensitive, and I'm sorry. It won't happen again."

The carefully professional expression on Michelle's face doesn't change, but the way her eyes blink tells me he's taken her by surprise. "Thank you, Nic. I accept your apology."

Nic smiles and gives her a quick nod.

Mike picks up his pen. "What do you got for us, Michelle?"

"I was able to develop a full autosomal DNA profile for your Cardinal Doe," she says. "I was a little worried when I received the specimens that they may be too degraded. Fortunately that was not the case. Your medical examiner is to be commended for their excellent condition after fifteen years in storage."

"Thank you," Mike says.

"I uploaded the profile to the OurDNA database."

"Did you get any matches?" Mike asks. *Click-click-click* goes his pen.

"The term 'match' is a bit of a misnomer," Michelle says. "In this context, these are people with whom your Cardinal Doe happens to share some DNA. The more DNA shared, the closer the relative. Many distant relatives, like half third cousins twice removed, are on her match list. They share a fraction of a percent of DNA with Cardinal Doe and aren't very useful. In forensic genetic genealogy cases like this one, we try to limit the relatives we investigate to second cousins or closer, or a minimum of one point five percent shared DNA. This dramatically increases the chance we'll find someone who can help identify a John or Jane Doe."

"What if the closest relative you can find is like a fourth cousin?" Nic asks. He's clearly very interested in this stuff. I can barely keep up.

"In that scenario we'll go back to the client and let them know that there isn't much we can do to help at this time. The number of DNA profiles in the databases is continually growing, so our advice usually is to wait a year or two and try again." Michelle briefly looks down, then back up at her camera. "Fortunately that is not the case with your Cardinal Doe."

Mike blows air out between his lips like he's been holding it for a long time.

"We found a female relative with about twenty-seven percent shared DNA with your Cardinal Doe," Michelle says. "That would be an aunt, a grandmother, a cousin, or possibly a half-sister."

"Whoa," Nic breathes. "That's a close relative."

Michelle nods. "According to OurDNA, her name is Victoria Reddick."

"I'll be goddamned," Mike says, wonder in his voice. "An actual, honest-to-god lead."

"Does it say where she's located?" Nic asks.

Michelle shakes her head. "Unfortunately, no."

"I guess you'll have to do some old-fashioned detective work to find her, Nic." Mike starts clicking his pen again.

"Give me a search engine and five minutes. I'll find her."

"Of course I'll send all the documentation over right away," Michelle says. "Do you need anything else from me?"

"I think we're good," Mike says. Emotion washes across his tired face. "Thank you, Michelle."

"Of course," she says, smiling. "Talk soon."

Mike ends the video call, then looks at Nic. "Want to see if we can find this Victoria Reddick?"

Nic scoots his chair closer to Mike's. "Hell yeah."

"All right." Mike pulls up his internet search engine, types in Victoria Reddick's name, and hits enter. They scroll through a few pages. "There doesn't seem to be too many people with that name," Mike says.

"And only one who is anywhere near us." Nic points at a listing close to the bottom of the screen. "This one is in Minneapolis."

Mike clicks into the listing and is rewarded with an address. "Just gonna print this," he mutters.

The printer in the bullpen spits out a sheet of paper. Nic grabs it and examines it. "What if I take a little road trip and meet Victoria in person? I have a cousin in Minneapolis I can stay with, it wouldn't cost the department anything except gas and maybe a couple of meals."

Mike considers this. "Normally I'd advocate for starting with a phone call, but in this case I think it's worth the expense. Bring me the paperwork and I'll sign it."

Nic stands. "You got it, boss."

After he leaves, Mike retrieves his recorder. "Mike Franklin, checking in. Today's date is Monday, August twelfth, ten-hundred hours. Just met with Nic Morris and Michelle Musgrove, who is from the private lab we're working with on your case. She must be some kind of magician, because she was able to use your DNA to dig up a lead. Michelle says this lady in Minneapolis is a pretty close relative of yours. A cousin or an aunt, most likely. I'm sending Nic to Minneapolis to track her down." He slides the bracelet toward him and covers it with his hand. "For fifteen years I've been saying I want your case solved. And I do, more than anything. But I'll tell you, it's killing me slowly inside that it won't be me who solves it. The Chief made it clear that I'm not allowed to ever work your case again – but right now that just feels like a hollow excuse. I should have tried harder."

I remember the day Mike came back from treatment and learned he would not be investigating Cardinal Doe anymore.

∞

"Ah, there you are."

I instantly spring awake. I know that voice. Mike's back!

I inspect him closely while he sets the Cardinal Doe case box on a table in the storage room and inspects its contents. He looks good. Refreshed. Clear-eyed. What a difference. He's a complete one-eighty from the shell of a man who hit rock bottom the day he showed up drunk to work.

Mike grunts, satisfied, and picks up the box. He's halfway to the bullpen when he encounters Chief Schmidt coming out of the men's room.

"What do you got there, Mike?" As if the Chief doesn't know exactly what Mike has in his hands.

"The Cardinal Doe case. Now that I'm back I'm ready to pick up where I left off."

"Let's take a walk to my office." Mike's shoulders drop a little as he follows the Chief. His office is big enough to hold a large desk, a tall bookshelf, and a round four-person conference table. Four big, sunny windows look out over the parking lot. Both men sit in adjoining chairs at the table, and Mike slides the box to the other side, out of the way.

Chief Schmidt gives Mike a frank look. "Been drinking at all?"

Mike holds his gaze. "No, sir. Ninety-five days sober. And counting."

"Good." The Chief points at the box. "Do you really think this is a good idea?"

"What do you mean?"

"Have you forgotten already what this case did to you? My god, man, you had to go to treatment for three months to get yourself right again."

"Aw, come on, Chief. It wasn't the case that did that. It was…" his voice trails off.

Chief Schmidt looks at Mike with kind, sympathetic eyes. I can barely see his lips moving under his mustache. "The case was your last straw. I know it, and you know it."

Mike looks down at his hands, which are twisting nervously in his lap.

"You were already having a tough time recovering from the trauma of losing your family. Then this case came along and sent you right off the rails." Chief Schmidt leans back in his chair and rests an ankle on a knee. "Did you know there's actually a term the shrinks use for this? It's called transference. That's when a person redirects their feelings about someone in their past to somebody else in the present. It happens between therapists and their patients a lot. You, though, you could never do something so predictable. You had to redirect your feelings about Rachel and Kylie onto an unidentified dead girl."

Mike tries to chuckle, but manages only a weak 'huh' sound.

"I blame myself. I should have known better than to let you take this case. So I'm going to do now what I should have done back in April. I cannot in good conscience allow you anywhere near Cardinal Doe."

Mike looks up, his blue eyes pleading. "Come on, Chief, she's what got me through treatment. I promised myself I would see it through when I came back. You gotta let me try again."

The Chief shakes his head. "She's what put you in treatment, Mike. No. I'm sorry."

"Well, is somebody gonna work it?"

"We're going to let Cardinal Doe sit for a while," the Chief says. "She's not going anywhere. If a lead magically appears in the meantime, we'll talk."

Mike is obviously disappointed, but knows better than to argue. "Can I keep the bracelet, anyway?"

"Just keep it in its case."

So my bracelet returns to its rightful place on Mike's desk and my case goes back to storage, where it sits untouched until Mike gets his promotion. That's when he realizes he now has a whole team of detectives who can investigate it for him, keeping him on the Chief's good side while also getting what he wants. Eric Plummer has the honor of being the first to try and fail, and the one to track the case file down in storage.

Since that day, even now, Mike keeps the case file locked up in his desk when his latest new detective isn't working on it.

He likes to keep me close.

∞

Mike picks the bracelet up and rubs his thumb gently over its clear plastic case. "But I think we're finally making some real progress," he says in a low voice. "I think this kid is finally gonna do what I couldn't."

I think he's right.

PART 2:
THE SECOND FAMILY

CHAPTER 9

Nic comes back some time later for what must be his regular weekly meeting with Mike. Mike is sitting in his chair, back to the door, staring unfocusedly at the Cardinal Doe sketch. He's been like this since he got here, later than usual. His eyes are dark-ringed and heavy-lidded; he clearly still isn't sleeping.

"Uh, boss?" Nic says tentatively. "Are you ready for me?"

Mike swivels to face him.

Nic blinks, a bit taken aback by his raggedy appearance. "Holy shit, are you all right?"

"I'm fine. Sit."

He sits. "You don't look fine. You look like you haven't slept in weeks."

Mike sighs deeply. "I haven't."

Nic frowns. "Why? Is it the case? If you're worried about Cardinal Doe, don't be. I got this."

"I know you do, Nic. It's not that. Well – okay, it is that, but not for the reason you're thinking." He pauses, debating how much he wants to say. "Cardinal Doe burrowed under my skin fifteen years ago and never left. Watching you make progress with our girl has been awesome – and really, really hard. I can't help but wonder if I tried hard enough back in '09."

"I read the case files back to front and inside out, boss. You did everything you could."

"Then why am I having dreams about running just one more missing persons search with a wider radius and boom, there she is? If I had expanded my radius back then, would I have ID'ed her?"

Nic shrugs. "Like I said, you did everything you could back in '09. I wouldn't have done anything different."

Mike rubs his hands over his face, then sighs. "This damn case is calling up some ghosts from my past that I would really rather not deal with."

"Even I know that ghosts don't go away until you deal with them." Nic sits back and places one ankle on the other knee. "And that's coming from someone who is not known for his high emotional intelligence."

Mike's eyebrows go up and a bemused smile plays at the corners of his lips. "I'll keep that in mind." He picks up his pen and starts clicking it. "Speaking of our girl, what's the latest? How was Minneapolis?"

Nic opens his laptop and consults his notes. "I paid Victoria Reddick a visit on Tuesday morning. She goes by Tori and lives in a subsidized apartment in northeast Minneapolis. She works full-time for a bookstore just down the street. I lucked out and caught her at home on her day off."

"What did she have to say?"

"I asked her about her family. No sisters, one brother. She does have one aunt, on her mother's side, a lady by the name of Anna Starkey. She is alive and well and living in Stillwater, Minnesota."

Mike nods slowly. "Not our Cardinal Doe, then."

"Nope."

"What else?" *Click-click-click.*

Nic goes back to his notes. "Tori told me her older brother Christian struggles with addiction and is transient. Couch-surfs, takes advantage of vulnerable and gullible women, like that. You know the type."

Mike nods.

"Christian stops by and sees Tori sometimes. She gives him food and lends an ear if he needs it, but refuses to give him money or allow him to stay with her. Smart." Nic scrolls. "Ah, let's see. Oh. She is currently not in contact with her mother. There seems to be bad blood there."

"Where's Dad?"

Nic looks up. "You're not gonna believe this, boss. Her father has been missing for thirty-three years."

Mike frowns. "Are you serious?"

Nic nods. "As a heart attack. Reid Reddick, that's Tori's dad, vanished from Minneapolis in May of 1991. Tori never knew him. That's why we found her DNA in the database. She did it about a year ago, hoping it might help her find her dad."

Mike ponders this. "Very interesting indeed." *Click-click-click.*

"What are you thinking, boss?"

"I'm thinking the odds of stumbling over a missing person while investigating a Jane Doe and the two cases not being related somehow are miniscule." Mike tosses his pen on his desk. "Take all of this to Michelle Musgrove and see what she might be able to do with it. If there's a connection, I'm betting she'll find it."

"Good call, boss. The whole thing feels kind of hinky to me too."

With that, Nic stands and gathers his laptop as Mike waves Jewel in for her weekly meeting. She and Nic exchange smiles as they pass each other in the doorway. It seems Eric was right, they are getting along well.

Too well, if you ask me.

"You're never going to believe this, boss." Jewel sits and opens her laptop. "I just talked to Patsy Finch. Remember I had concerns about the DNA report from the DOJ on the Allie Bergstrom case?"

Mike nods. "Yeah, it didn't line up with your evidence."

"Right. I took it to Patsy like you recommended. Dr. Ferrell refused to make a determination and asked crime lab leadership to investigate further. Patsy just called to tell me that they reviewed the DNA analyst's work and they think they've uncovered a pattern of misconduct going back years. She thinks hundreds of cases could be compromised."

Mike sits back in his chair and gives a low whistle. "Holy shit."

Jewel nods. "Yeah. Murders, assaults, rapes, child sexual assaults…all are going to have to be reviewed and probably retested."

"There could be innocent people sitting in prison." Mike's eyes are wide.

"And guilty people walking free. Yeah, it's a huge mess."

"I assume this means your gut was right? That Jamison Downey was, in fact, driving the car when it crashed and killed Allie Bergman?"

"Patsy hasn't come out and said those exact words, but that's the impression I get."

Mike ponders this. "I still think Jamison's father might have had something to do with it. Maybe our DNA analyst is susceptible to bribery? Or blackmail?"

"Maybe. In the meantime, I still have an active investigation and Jamison already has a defense attorney who is sharp as tacks. About as friendly, too."

"We need to get the DNA retested."

"Yes. I'd like to send it to the lab in Madison if I could. I think Wausau's going to be mired in this thing for a long time and I don't want my case to suffer for it."

"Fair enough. I'll call Chuck." Chuck Rasmussen is the administrator of the DOJ's Division of Forensic Sciences. Mike jots a note in his battered notebook. "He owes me a favor. Worst case, we hire a private lab. But I don't think it'll come to that."

Jewel thanks him and gathers up her things.

"Before you go, can I ask you a question?" Mike asks.

"Of course, boss."

"How are things going with Nic? Any better?"

"Much better," she says with a nod. "I don't know what you said to him, but he's been much more pleasant to be around."

"I threatened him with his job. Reminded him that he's still on probation and he'd better shape up or he's out."

"So far he seems to be shaping up," Jewel says, and leaves.

Mike goes out to the pen to grab a cup of coffee. When he returns, he closes the door behind him and pulls his recorder out of his bag. "Mike Franklin, checking in. Today's date is Thursday, August fifteenth, oh-nine-thirty hours. Didn't sleep much again last night. If I'm not dreaming about Rachel and Kylie, I'm dreaming about you. Last night I dreamt that I was back in 2009, investigating your case, and when I searched the missing persons database, I set the search radius to two hundred miles instead of one hundred. Lo and behold, there you were, and your photo matched my sketch perfectly." His forehead furrows a bit. "I couldn't see the name, though. It was blurry. And when I woke up, I couldn't shake the feeling that I'd missed something in my original investigation. Why didn't I search again and expand the radius after I eliminated Jo Ann Payton and Taylor Bresette? What if the opportunity to identify you was right there and I ignored it?" He sips his coffee. "I hate thinking that we're still spinning our wheels now, fifteen years later, because I didn't do something simple and obvious back then. It kinda eats me up." He sighs. "Let it go, Mike, let it go. Nic's making some real progress. Be happy about that." He pours some more coffee down his gullet, then says something alarming. "God, I'm just so tired. And I could really use a drink." Then, as if he didn't just drop the mother of all bombs, he nonchalantly tosses the recorder back in his bag and turns to face his computer.

Oh, no. No no no, this can't be happening. If he's thinking about a drink, that means his mental health is bad enough to put his sobriety at risk. If he were to lose that, everything he's worked so hard for the last fifteen years would be in jeopardy. He almost lost it all once.

Toward the end of his time investigating my case, right around the time he hung up on Kristina Baldwin when she accosted him with questions about his family, he started drinking pretty much all the time. He would fill a travel coffee mug from a nearby convenience store with whiskey every morning and carry it around with him, taking nips throughout the day. He also kept a supply of cherry-flavored cough drops in his pants pockets. He thought he was hiding it so well.

News flash: he wasn't.

∞

It's late on a Friday afternoon when Pete Mumford and Maggie Conover approach Mike's desk with worried looks on their faces. Their concern is justified; Mike is sitting there staring glassily at his computer, the Cardinal Doe sketch in one hand and his white plastic travel mug gripped tightly in the other.

Pete stops short a few steps away from Mike and waves a fat hand in front of his beefy face. "Jesus. He smells like a distillery."

Maggie squats next to Mike. "Whatcha got in the cup, Mike?"

Mike's head swivels in Maggie's general direction and a sloppy smile crosses his face. "Oh, hi Maggie. Iss juss a drink." His words slur together.

Maggie pries the cup out of Mike's fingers. He doesn't resist, just watches with huge fuzzy eyes. He's way more intoxicated than I realized.

Maggie sniffs the cup and cringes. "Whiskey." She takes the top off and peeks inside. "Not much left. And this is a forty-ounce cup." She looks at Mike, her eyes wide.

"Jesus Christ," Pete mutters. "That's more than a liter."

Maggie squats next to Mike again. "I'm going to hang on to this, okay? And Pete is going to take you home."

"Um." This seems to confuse him, and his brow furrows. "Okay."

Pete helps Mike stand and guides him out of the bullpen. Maggie follows, still holding Mike's cup. I suspect she's going to talk to the Chief.

My suspicion is confirmed on Monday morning. Mike comes in early as usual, and is looking at my bracelet when his desk phone rings.

"Franklin. Oh, hey, Chief, how—" He listens. "Okay. Yes, I'm on my way." He sets the phone back in its cradle and sighs deeply. He knows he's in trouble. He absentmindedly sticks the bracelet in his pants pocket as he makes his way to the Chief's office. I follow along behind him.

He stops in front of the Chief's open office door and knocks lightly on the doorjamb. Schmidt waves him in. "Close the door and have a seat."

Mike does as he's told.

The Chief opens a desk drawer, pulls out Mike's travel mug, and sets it on the desk between them. "That look familiar to you, Mike?"

Mike's eyes widen in shock. He realizes he's been busted, despite all his clever methods for hiding his drinking from his colleagues. "Uh. Yes, sir, it's mine. I—"

Schmidt holds a hand up. "Do us both a favor and save it."

Mike's mouth snaps shut like a trap.

"Maggie brought this to me on Friday after Pete drove you home. She said you were so wasted you could barely string a sentence together."

Mike's whole head turns red and his gaze drops to the floor.

"You're drinking on the job, and now I've got a problem. I have about seven different policy manuals that tell me you're a danger to the community and I should take your badge and gun on the spot."

Mike's head pops up. His eyes are round and panicked.

"Do you have anything to say for yourself?"

Mike clears his throat. "No, other than I realize I fucked up, and I'm sorry."

Schmidt gazes at Mike with sad eyes. "I don't want to shitcan you, Mike. I hired you specifically because I believe you have the potential to not only be an excellent detective, but maybe even lead Investigations someday. Roger Nichols is already making noises about retirement. Something about a boat and the Florida Keys." He waves a hand in the air as if Captain Nichols and his retirement dreams are some kind of bothersome fly. "But I should. This kind of reckless behavior is unacceptable. I won't tolerate it."

"I understand." Mike's shoulders slump and his back hunches. He's preparing himself for the final painful blow.

"So, against my better judgment, I'm going to give you one more chance to show me you have what it takes to do this job."

Mike suddenly sits up straight. "Thank you, Chief, I–"

Schmidt holds a hand up again and Mike shuts up. "Don't thank me yet, because there are conditions. You are to abstain from alcohol. If I or anyone else in the department ask to inspect your drink container, you will comply. And you will check in with me daily. If you fail to meet any of these conditions, you're done. Am I making myself perfectly clear?"

Mike nods. "Yes, sir."

"Don't let me down, Mike. Don't let your team down."

"I won't."

∞

He would. And when he did, Chief Schmidt once again decided to help him rather than punish him. He must have truly seen Mike's potential, just like Mike sees Nic's.

But the Chief's help comes with conditions, and his goodwill only goes so far. If Mike gets caught drinking again, he'll be out on his ass. If that happens and he misses out on the resolution of the Cardinal Doe case…well, let's just say I don't know that he would survive that.

He needs to control his urge to drink.

Mike refills his coffee and stifles a yawn as he moves on to his next meeting.

Just another day in paradise.

CHAPTER 10

It's late. The sky outside Mike's office window is the color of charcoal and nobody is around. Mike went home hours ago. Or so I thought. Imagine my surprise when he walks into his office dressed in street clothes – t-shirt, shorts, and sandals – and carrying his work bag.

What is he doing?

He sits in his chair, sets his bag between his feet, and pulls out a pint bottle of bourbon.

Oh my god. He's in worse shape than I realized.

Mike examines the bottle for a long time. He hefts it in his hands. He puts on his glasses and reads both labels in their entirety. He presses the unopened cap to his nose as if sniffing its aromas. It's like he's getting reacquainted with an old friend.

Except this is no friend. It almost destroyed him once.

I expect him to open the bottle, but he doesn't. Instead he stashes it in a desk drawer and locks it, then walks out with the key. He has no key when he returns, and I wonder what he did with it. He grabs his bag, turns off his office light, and leaves.

One little key is the only thing separating Mike from temptation now. It's only a matter of time until he won't be able to resist. I worry that if he relapses, he may not make it through this time.

And then I realize: maybe that's the whole point.

CHAPTER 11

A long time passes before Nic Morris comes back to Mike's office to talk about Cardinal Doe. In the meantime Mike and his team go about the business of catching bad guys. Mike is still not sleeping, but he's also not talking about nightmares. That feels like a little progress, anyway.

He pushes through each day despite his exhaustion. He continues to resist the urge to pull that bottle of whiskey out of his desk drawer. I'm super proud of him, but I'm not convinced he can hold out forever. I've seen him longingly gaze at that drawer.

He's doing that right now, as a matter of fact. I wonder where he goes when he zones out like that. Is he imagining how his first sip of whiskey will taste? Does he remember how it feels going down? Does he look forward to being overwhelmed by sweet waves of numbness so he doesn't have to feel anymore? I don't know for sure, but I have my suspicions.

Nic appears at Mike's door and knocks. "You ready, boss?"

Mike blinks and turns to his computer to start a video meeting. "Let's do it."

Michelle Musgrove appears, says hello, and gets right to the point. "I'm working on building a family tree for Cardinal Doe.

Here, let me share my screen." Michelle's face is replaced with a graphic that doesn't really look like a tree. It's horizontal instead of vertical and it's a maze of names in boxes with lines connecting them.

"As you can see, this is Victoria Reddick's family tree," Michelle says. And now I understand what I'm looking at. Victoria's name is in one of two solitary boxes on the left side of the graphic. Her brother's name, Christian Reddick, is just above hers, and her father's name, Reid Reddick, to the right. Just below Reid is the name Susan Starkey; that must be Victoria's mother. A line connects Reid and Susan to Christian and Victoria. Each level of boxes that branches to the right is another generation, and the names double in number. Michelle had been able to trace four generations back so far; the names on the far right of the graphic are so small they're almost unreadable.

"And this is what I have so far for Cardinal Doe." A new family tree graphic replaces Victoria's. It is empty, save for Cardinal Doe's name in a box on the far left. An untethered box to the right has Victoria Reddick's name in it. "Victoria Reddick is the only genetic relative I've found that is close enough to Cardinal Doe for analysis. They share a significant amount of DNA, just over two thousand centimorgans." The basically blank page disappears, replaced by Michelle's sober face. "I should be able to connect them, and I can't."

"Tori's only aunt is alive," Nic says. "So we know she's not Cardinal Doe. What were the other possible relationships you mentioned, Michelle?"

Michelle's eyes move away from her camera as she looks at something else. "A first cousin, a grandparent, or a half-sibling could share around 25% of DNA." She looks back at the camera.

"Can you pull up Tori's tree again?" Nic asks.

Michelle obliges. Nic leans forward to get a better look. "I don't see that Tori has any cousins."

"Correct," Michelle confirms. She looks down and reads from something in front of her. "Reid Reddick is, or was, an only child, and both of his parents were gone by the mid-eighties. Susan Reddick has a sister, who is unmarried and childless. Her father passed away in 1993 and her mother died five years ago." Michelle looks up again. "Nobody in Victoria's family tree fits the profile, and the timing doesn't line up."

Mike makes a fist and bounces it on his desk. "So what are we missing here?"

Michelle shrugs. "DNA doesn't lie. Victoria Reddick and Cardinal Doe are related. There's no question about that. The only possibility I can think of is that someone along the line changed their name. That would make it difficult, if not impossible, to find them using conventional genealogy methods."

The conference ends and Nic sighs and falls back against his chair like a balloon losing its air. "Great. A dead end."

Mike's computer dings; Michelle has sent over the family trees and her reports. Mike pulls up the Reddick family tree and examines it again. "Maybe not."

Nic sits up straight again. "What do you mean?"

Mike swivels in his chair to face Nic. "I mean, the genetic genealogy might not have given us the answers we were hoping for, but we're not done yet." He points to Reid Reddick's name.

"This guy is missing, and now we know he's somehow related to our girl. I want to know everything about him. We're going to run him down until we either get something helpful or there's nothing left to chase." He gives Nic a hard look, his eyes dark and heavy. "I don't believe in coincidences."

Nic understands the assignment. "Looks like I'm headed back to Minneapolis, huh?"

"Go to Minneapolis, get your hands on the Reid Reddick missing person report, and do some digging. Find out what happened and what, if anything, Minneapolis has done to find him. And what the status of the case is now."

"I'm on it," Nic said. "I'll have Cora pull the files for me so they're waiting when I get there."

Mike eyebrows shoot up. "Oh? Who's Cora?"

Nic's ears turn pink. "She's the Minneapolis detective who helped me track down Victoria Reddick." He tries to hide a smile and fails. First he wins Jewel over, and now there's a Cora? My boyfriend gets around.

"Keep me posted," Mike says.

Nic leaves with a nod. Mike stands and goes to the door. "Roy! A word, please."

Jewel follows him into the office. "Door open or closed?"

"Closed." Mike sits.

Jewel closes the door and also sits. "What's up, boss?"

"Things still good with Nic?"

Jewel grins. "All good, boss. I think his change of heart is actually going to stick. He likes it here too much to screw it up."

"I'm glad to hear it," Mike says, clearly pleased.

"Need anything else?"

"Nope, that's it. Thanks, Jewel."

She leaves and Mike digs out his recorder. "Mike Franklin, checking in. Today's date is Monday, August nineteenth, twelve-thirty hours. I'm sending Nic back to Minneapolis to track down the mysterious Reid Reddick. I think he's going to be the key to solving your case." He pauses, thinking. "I had some doubts about Nic for a while there, but he's turning out to be a gem. I'm very pleased with his progress, both on your case and on his behavior. The team seems to be embracing him, which is extremely cool." He gives a low chuckle. "I feel…validated. Like I made the right decision for once."

He turns the device off and stashes it back in his bag. Then he turns his attention to other things.

There really is no rest for the weary.

CHAPTER 12

It's dark, it's quiet, and everyone has gone home after another long, chaotic day. Everyone but Mike, apparently; here he is, walking back into his office after disappearing for a bit. He's carrying a white coffee mug with the Superior Police Department badge printed on it. He sets it on his desk and goes back to close and lock the door. He makes sure the sidelight window next to the door is covered. Then he returns to his desk and fishes something out of his pants pocket: a key. I realize with growing dread that it's the key to the locked desk drawer where he keeps the bourbon. Sure enough, he uses it and within seconds he's lifting the bottle from the drawer. His handsome face is determined, his mouth set in a thin straight line. Yet the shame in his eyes is unmistakable. He is fully aware he's about to make what could end up being the worst mistake of his life – but he can't stop himself from doing it.

Mike quickly removes the cap from the bottle and pours amber liquid into the mug, as if he's afraid he might chicken out. The bottle's glass neck clinks nervously against the ceramic. He recaps the bottle and sets it aside, then carefully lifts the mug to his face. Panic crashes over me. I so badly want to slap that mug right out of his hand. I know I have no voice, but that doesn't stop me from trying to scream at him: *No! Don't do it, Mike! You'll regret it forever!*

His breath catches in his throat and his back straightens. Did he…did he hear me? No. No way. That's impossible. Isn't it?

"I don't know what else to do," he says in a low voice. Does he know I'm here, listening? "The nightmares about Rachel and Kylie are getting worse. This morning I woke up convinced that I'd killed them myself." He takes a deep, uneven breath. "I didn't. I just wasn't there to save them, to stop Rachel. And that's exactly how she planned it." A long pause as Mike works to control his emotions. "If I'm not dreaming about them, I'm dreaming about you. I didn't realize it would be this soul-crushing to watch another detective do the job that I should have done fifteen years ago. Whether I'm at work or at home, doesn't matter what I do, I'm a fucking failure." A deep, gut-wrenching sob escapes him. "I don't sleep. God, I just need to turn it all off and *sleep.*"

No. I watch helplessly as he tips his head back and sends that shot of bourbon down his gullet. He grimaces and sets the mug on his desk, then closes his eyes and props his head in his hands. He sits like that for a long time, silent. I wait anxiously to see if he decides to pour himself another shot. He doesn't. Eventually he stands, puts the bottle in his bag, grabs the mug, and leaves.

All I can do is hope he didn't just wake up his demon.

CHAPTER 13

It's business as usual at the Superior Police Department's Investigations unit while Nic is in Minneapolis. Jewel Roy is waiting not-so-patiently for the results of a second test on the DNA from her vehicular homicide case. Eric Plummer is still trying to sort out the scope of Dooley Wallace's latest fraud. They, along with Simon Griffith and Maggie Conover, juggle full caseloads as well. Mike Franklin supervises his team while performing his administrative duties – and mustering every last bit of strength he has to hold himself together.

That strength is fading fast. This morning he came to work looking not only exhausted, but hung over. I know what that looks like; the sunken eyes, parched lips, and stubble on his face are a dead giveaway. Every day started like this toward the end of his time with the Cardinal Doe case.

Mike closes his door and pulls out his recorder. "Mike Franklin, checking in. Today's date is Monday, August twenty-sixth, oh-eight-hundred hours. The nightmares continue. It's impossible to sleep. Every time I try, I wake up screaming." He thinks for a moment, then: "Last night I dreamed about finding Kylie dead in the bathtub. Again. But this time I didn't wake up at that point. Oh, no. No, the fun continued. I left the bathroom and went into the master bedroom looking for Rachel. I noticed a window was open. I leaned out and looked down…and there she was, lying on the patio, her head cocked at an unnatural angle and a huge pool of blood underneath her." Another long pause. "My hands felt sticky when I lifted them from the window frame. I looked at them and they were drenched in blood. That's when I woke up screaming." He takes a deep breath. "I didn't even try to go back to sleep after that. There's no way that was happening.

"I thought I had this beat," he says, frustration vibrating in his voice. "I was doing okay until I handed Nic the Cardinal Doe case. He's going to solve it, there's no doubt in my mind. You will finally get your name back. It's what I've always wanted. More than anything. So why is this such a struggle for me?"

He thinks for a bit, rubbing his grizzled face with his hands, and then he says something that surprises me. "God, maybe Nic's right. Ghosts don't go away until you deal with them. It seems I still have some work to do." He stops recording and picks up the phone. When someone answers he says, "Cheryl, it's Mike. I need a few minutes of Paul's time this week." He listens, and nods, says "Thank you," and hangs up.

There's a knock at the door. Mike hides his recorder and rearranges himself at his desk. "Come on in."

Nic appears holding his laptop and a cardboard box. "Ready for me, boss?"

"Yep. How was Minneapolis?"

Nic sits. "Productive," he says as he sets the box to the side and opens his laptop.

"Let's hear it."

"All right. The first thing I did was get the Reid Reddick missing person case files from Cora and read through them. In 1991 Reid was a financial advisor with a successful practice in Northeast Minneapolis. He'd been married to his wife Susan for fifteen years. They had one child, ten-year-old Christian, and a baby on the way, due in October. That would be Tori. They had a nice house not too far from his office, two nice cars, white picket fence, the whole bit."

Mike nodded, listening.

"On May twenty-fifth Susan took Christian up north to a resort on Catclaw Lake for Memorial Day weekend. Reid was to drive up and join them the following day, Sunday. He never showed. Susan tried calling him at home and at his office all day, and he never answered."

"Before cellphones," Mike says, almost to himself.

"Right. When Reid didn't show at the resort by Monday morning, Susan packed up Christian and their stuff and rushed back to Minneapolis. They arrived home to find the house exactly as they'd left it. All of Reid's things were there, nothing was disturbed, nothing was missing. The only thing out of the ordinary was that Reid's wallet was sitting on the kitchen counter with ID, credit cards, and cash inside. His Audi was in the garage with the keys in it. Susan called 911 and reported Reid missing. He hasn't been seen or heard from since."

Mike picked up his pen and started clicking it. "Sounds to me like someone who disappeared voluntarily."

"That's what MPD thought too. They took the report but didn't investigate at all. They told Susan that Reid was an adult and had the right to be missing if he wanted to be. The officer who took the report even wrote that in there. They said they couldn't spare the resources to investigate unless and until there was evidence of a crime."

Mike winces. "They did things differently in the nineties," he says.

"Yeah, that and the violent crime rate in Minneapolis that year was at an all-time high. MPD literally didn't have the resources to spare. Something had to give, I guess." Nic clicks to another page. "So then I tracked down Susan Reddick. She's remarried, goes by Susan Kline, lives in a trailer park in Saint Anthony Village. I swear, boss, I have never met an angrier, more bitter old lady in my life."

"Did she talk to you?" Mike asks.

"Not at first. She shut the door in my face as soon as I said 'Nic Morris with the Superior Police Department.' I had to call Cora. Mrs. Kline let us in when Cora introduced herself as Minneapolis police and told her we wanted to talk about Reid."

"What did she have to say?"

"Mostly what I already knew from the missing person report. Although she did mention one – no, two interesting things." Nic holds up one pointer finger. "First. She said that Reid Reddick was a self-absorbed and neglectful husband and father, but an excellent provider. She and Christian never wanted for anything, and Susan was able to be a stay-at-home mom. Which was extremely unfortunate when Reid disappeared and she was forced to support herself and her young son."

"Let me guess," Mike broke in. "No job skills or experience, no idea how to manage money."

"Bingo. That stress on top of the utter devastation of her husband disappearing without a trace isn't good for a pregnant woman."

Mike winces. "The baby."

"Came eight weeks early and spent a month in the NICU. To this day Tori still deals with some long-term effects of her premature birth: dyslexia, asthma, severe anxiety. Although I'm sure the environment she grew up in contributed to the anxiety too."

"Say more."

Nic raises his middle finger to make a peace sign. "Second. According to Mrs. Kline, her two ungrateful brats claim that her husband Tom, a retired heavy equipment operator and active blackout drunk, abused them growing up. She denies it, won't even entertain the idea. Never mind that both of her upper arms are covered in bruises that look suspiciously like fingertips that dug in too hard, and her front teeth appear to be veneers or a bridge."

Mike nods; he's familiar with the type. "Like her real teeth got knocked out of her head at some point."

"Right. So she claims that Tom kicked Christian out of the house shortly after his seventeenth birthday and she never hears from him. She doesn't seem too upset about it, either."

"And Tori?"

"Susan says that Tori never stopped lying about Tom abusing her, right up until the day she went to her brother's apartment and stayed gone. Tori was fourteen years old when she left and went no contact. Susan says good riddance."

"Jesus Christ," Mike mutters.

"I know. What's crazy is that Tori lives ten minutes from her mother. They haven't spoken in years."

"I assume you paid Tori a visit as well?" Mike asked.

"Yes, she was my next stop after Susan Kline kicked me and Cora out of her shitty trailer. It stank like mouse shit and cigarettes." Nic pinched his lips together and puffed his cheeks out a little to look like he might throw up.

"What did Tori have to say?"

"She is absolutely adamant that Tom Kline physically abused both her and Christian. Christian tried to protect Tori by taking the brunt of it. She was on her own after Christian left, and that bastard almost put her in the hospital twice." Nic pauses. "She says he sexually abused her too, and that's what really pissed Susan off. As if she regarded her own daughter as competition for her man's affections. So sick."

Click-click-click goes Mike's pen, faster now.

"But get this. According to Tori, she and Christian lived with their grandmother for two years after she was born. She doesn't remember it, but Christian is ten years older than she is and always talks about how good life was there."

"Susan couldn't hack it," Mike says.

"Exactly. She pawned the kids off on her mom so she could go out drinking and generally ignore her responsibilities. In fact, that's where she met Tom Kline. At the bar. And when she married Tom Kline, she took her kids back."

Mike pondered this. "Christian must have been, what, twelve or thirteen years old by this point? Plenty old enough to have an opinion."

"Yes. He was dead set against his mom marrying this creep, and Grandma had a few things to say about it too. She wanted custody but couldn't afford to fight for it in the courts. So in the end, Mom got the kids back and they all lived unhappily ever after. I find it interesting that Susan mentioned none of this when I talked to her."

"She's not going to admit that she's a terrible mother," Mike points out.

"True," Nic admits. "She's going to blame all of her kids' problems on the kids themselves, and on Reid."

Mike sits back in his chair, pen in fist, thumb poised over the plunger. "So what's next?"

"I tried to find Christian but had no luck," Nic says. "Tori doesn't know where he's living at the moment. Sometimes he shows up at her door when he needs something. She said she would call me next time he comes around. I did, however, find two of Reid Reddick's former employees."

Mike leans his elbows on his desk. "Remind me what he did for a living."

"Financial advisor," Nic says. "And a successful one, by all appearances. He had a beautiful office in Northeast Minneapolis by the river and more than five hundred million dollars in assets under management. He was one of the top performers at his firm."

"Any financial problems?" Mike asks.

"Not according to the woman who managed his office for him. Heather Buchanan. She doesn't remember seeing anything suspicious before Reid went missing. Neither does his junior associate, Mark Gallagher. All they know is they showed up for work on May twenty-eighth, the day after Memorial Day 1991, to find the office dark and the doors locked. Heather managed payroll for Reid and called the bank to find all of his accounts had nothing in them but mothballs. That's when they knew they were suddenly unemployed."

"I'm still feeling like Reid skipped town of his own accord," Mike says.

"I thought so too, and figured there had to be more to the story. I asked Heather if there was anyone in the firm who supervised Reid," Nic says. "She gave me the name and number of his field leader, John Farmer. And boy, did he have a story to tell. Apparently Reddick had been fraudulently helping himself to his clients' money for *years*. Government regulators and the FBI were sniffing around and his firm had opened an investigation when he vanished."

"How much money are we talking about?"

"Several million, easy," Nic says. "Plenty enough to support a lifestyle where the wife doesn't have to work and the kid never wants for anything."

Mike gives a low whistle. "What happened to the assets he was managing?"

"Reddick only took the money he had in his own bank accounts and left his clients' assets untouched. Farmer told me the firm assigned his clients and his office personnel – Heather and Mark – to other advisors. The firm and the FBI are very interested to know where Reddick is."

"I bet they are." Mike points at the box Nic brought with him. "What's in there?"

Nic slides the box toward him. "Some items that Farmer kept from Reddick's office. He figured the family would want it, but nobody ever picked it up. Having met Reddick's wife, it makes sense."

Nic pulls the box flaps apart and both men peer inside. Nic reaches in and pulls out a framed family photo: the man has thinning brown hair, a mustache that curls over his top lip, and heavy plastic-framed glasses; the woman has a thousand-watt smile, a fresh blonde perm, and a wide-collared shirtdress; and the young boy sports a long Cousin Oliver bowl haircut. The frame is ornate and made of metal, and the photo inside looks like it had been taken at the local department store sometime in the early 1980s. The colors are badly faded, mostly orange and yellow tones now.

"There's Susan, much younger and less wrinkled, and looking only slightly less batshit," Nic says. "This is the Family Reddick." He sets the photo aside.

I'm powerfully drawn to the father in the photo. Reid Reddick. There's something about his deeply set eyes and thin, straight nose that seems to tug at a long-hidden memory. I'd never heard his name before Nic started working the Cardinal Doe case, but there's something about the man. I wish I could remember.

Mike draws another framed photo from the box, examines it for a moment, then turns it so Nic can see. This photo is newer than the family portrait, showing a slightly older Reid Reddick grinning and shaking hands with a tall, trim man in neatly pressed khaki pants with feathered brown hair that touched the collar of his expensive blue polo shirt. The frame is shiny silver and the words MILLION DOLLAR CLUB 1989 are engraved along the bottom in a loopy script. "There's two more."

Nic pulls them out; they're identical to the first photo save for the year (one is from 1986 and the other from 1984) and the man in the photo with Reddick. 1986 is a tall man in a gray suit, glasses, and a square-shaped combover hairstyle. 1984 features a squat older bald man with a liver-spotted scalp, the deepest wrinkles I've ever seen on a human face, and crooked, coffee-stained teeth.

"What's the Million Dollar Club?" Mike wonders.

"I don't know, but I know who might," Nic says. "Heather Buchanan, Reddick's office manager."

Mike nods as he places the framed photos back inside the box. "Well then, you know what to do next."

"You got it, boss." Nic stands, gathers up his laptop and the box, and leaves Mike's office.

Mike turns his attention to his computer and catches up on emails until the phone rings. He picks it up. "Franklin. Hey, Paul. Sure. I'm on my way."

True to his word, he puts the phone back on its cradle and leaves his office.

An impromptu meeting with the Chief. I wish I could tag along.

CHAPTER 14

Nic comes back to Mike's office with an update later the very same day. Mike's just hanging up the phone when Nic appears at his door holding a sheet of printer paper. "Come on in," he says and rubs his face.

Nic takes his usual chair. "Everything all right, boss?"

"Yeah. I'm good. What do you got?"

"I scanned those photos and sent them to Heather Buchanan. She says the Million Dollar Club were people who became millionaires while they were clients of Reid Reddick."

Mike tents his fingers in front of his lips, but doesn't say anything.

"Reddick big-dealed these guys, threw each of them a lavish party at a swanky restaurant. He invited their friends and family, and other high-net-worth clients of his. It was like he was showing off, you know? Wanted them to see what he could do for them."

"And broke every gifting rule in the book doing it," Mike murmurs.

Nic chuckles. "Probably. Reddick would hire a photographer to take pictures at these parties, always making sure there was one of him shaking the new millionaire's hand. He'd put that photo in a fancy frame and give it to them. Apparently he kept one for himself as well. Probably so he could hang them in his office."

"Did Heather tell you who these clients were?"

"Yes." Nic looks down at his printout. "1984 was a local physician named Frederick Harmon. 1986 was a fellow by the name of Lloyd Maines. He was the CEO of a manufacturing company just down the street from Reid's office."

Maines. *Maines.* The name floats effortlessly through my consciousness, as if it belongs there. I feel like I should know it, just like I thought I should know Reid Reddick's face. I try to follow it, and it leads me to the same writhing mass of unadulterated terror.

Oh god oh god—I can't breathe.

I'm forced to retreat. The Maines name remains a familiar mystery.

Nic continues. "And 1989, the younger guy, is David Thomas. Heather thinks he was a lobbyist of some sort, but couldn't remember for sure."

"And now it's your job to find out," Mike says.

"On it, boss."

Nic gathers up his stuff and leaves, trying to hold everything against his side with one arm as he closes the door behind him. A muted crash seconds later tells me he didn't get to his desk before gravity won and his precarious load fell to the floor.

Mike spends a minute or two searching for his recorder, finally finding it in a desk drawer. He presses the button and says, "Mike Franklin, checking in again. Nic's making solid progress on your case, and I'll be honest, I'm struggling. Hard. Am I jealous? Fuck yeah, I am. It should be *me*." He pauses for a long time, then: "I'm doing it again. Like every good selfish guy does, I'm making this about me, when it should be about her. The only difference is, this time it's my unidentified dead girl instead of my wife. What the hell is wrong with me? Why do I do this?" He runs a hand over his tired face. "I talked to the Chief. The man is a saint. He recommended a good therapist in Duluth and told me I should consider having Maggie oversee Nic's investigation." He sighs. "I hate that idea. I think it would somehow be worse to have no involvement at all. So I'll continue watching from the sidelines and cheering Nic on. Maybe soon I'll fucking get over myself and actually mean it." His exasperation is clear on his face as he tosses the recorder into his bag.

So that's what his meeting with the Chief was all about. For the first time since I've known him, Mike is voluntarily seeking help. He recognizes that Nic's investigation is causing him to regress, putting his sobriety at risk. And he's actively seeking the help he so desperately needs.

I couldn't be more proud of him.

CHAPTER 15

When Mike strolls into his office, I examine him closely. His brown hair is freshly cut, his goatee is perfectly trimmed, and the circles under his blue eyes seem a little less prominent. He looks like a man who maybe got a decent night's sleep.

He picks up the bracelet in its acrylic case and gazes at it for a few seconds, then sets it aside as Nic arrives for his usual meeting. He carries his laptop and all three Million Dollar Club photos in both arms like a watermelon. "You're never going to believe what I found, boss."

Mike can't hide a smile; Nic really does look goofy carrying his stuff like that. "Oh?"

Nic takes his seat and sets his load in front of him. "Okay. So I ran down the Million Dollar Club, and I think I may have finally caught a break."

Mike picks up his pen and leans back in his chair. "All right, lay it on me."

Nic holds up the 1984 photo of the older bald man with crooked teeth. I take a closer look and see a joviality and friendliness in the old man's face that I hadn't noticed before because I couldn't get over how wrinkled it was. "This here is Doctor Frederick Harmon. He was a respected pediatric surgeon at Children's Hospital in Minneapolis. He and his wife Joan never had any children of their own, but they dedicated their time and their money to making the lives of local children better. Joan chaired the hospital's foundation for many years, and together the Harmons supported numerous related charities. In fact, in the seventies they were mostly responsible for funding construction of a brand-new residential facility for families of children undergoing treatment at the hospital. It was cutting-edge at the time."

"Impressive," Mike says. "But no kids."

"Right. And both Fred and Joan have long since passed. Fred died in 1999 at the age of seventy-nine. Joan passed away in 2003, age eighty-three. Their estate continues to support the Children's Minnesota Foundation."

"All right, we can clear them. What else?"

Nic sets down the Harmon photo and picks up the one dated 1989. The man in this photo is significantly younger, with a perfect Miami Vice tan to go with his feathered mullet and teeth so white they dazzled. "This is David Thomas, highly successful agriculture lobbyist and lifelong bachelor."

"No kids?" Mike asks.

Nic shakes his head. "No kids. When he wasn't in Washington strong-arming Congress to pass bills friendly to Minnesota farmers, David was traveling the world looking for adventure. In June 1992, just three years after making his first million with Reddick, he was lost at sea while sailing along the California coast. His catamaran was found unmanned and floating about three miles off Catalina Island. He was declared dead by a judge in 1994. He would have been fifty-three years old."

"I'm beginning to suspect you've saved the best for last." Mike's pen starts clicking rapidly.

Nic sets David's photo aside and picks up the third one. "Lloyd Maines. CEO of Sprayko Incorporated, Minneapolis, from 1978 to 1990."

"He looks the part," Mike comments. And he's right. Lloyd's hair, a steely gray that matched his suit perfectly, is combed back from his face in a square-ish shape. His white shirt is perfectly pressed and his maroon tie is wide and straight. Gold square-framed glasses dominate his face.

Nic nods in agreement. "He'd been with the company since he graduated from high school in 1940. Married his wife Beverly shortly after he started working there in the logistics department."

Mike's eyebrows go up; his interest is piqued. "Any kids?"

"Two," Nic confirms. "A daughter, Jodi, and a son, Daniel. I tracked Jodi down and gave her a call. Her name is Cassel now. She told me her parents are both gone now and her brother Daniel died in 1989. Motorcycle crash."

"That's tough," Mike says.

"Yeah. He was on his way home after working the second shift as a forklift operator and a semi sideswiped his sport bike on Interstate 35W."

Mike winces.

"Jodi said her parents were never the same after losing their son. She's convinced they both died of a broken heart."

Mike doesn't say anything.

"After I hung up with Jodi I ran an internet search for Daniel Maines' name, hoping to find a news article or something with more details about his accident. I know 1989 was a long time ago, but you never know unless you try, right?"

Mike opens his mouth, but Nic is excited and doesn't give him a chance to speak.

"Remember the break I mentioned?" Nic types something and taps his laptop's trackpad as he speaks. "This is what I got when I searched Daniel Maines' name." He turns the computer around so Mike can see the screen.

Mike leans forward and squints, then grabs his readers and slides them onto his nose. On the screen is a website for a business called Foundations Wealth Advisors, based in a city called Caribou Creek, Minnesota. And right there in the middle of the homepage is a photo of a much older Reid Reddick, looking all professional and trustworthy in a black suit and striped tie. His hair, already thinning in his family portrait from the 1980s, is almost entirely gone now. What's left is white and shaved close to his head. Frameless eyeglasses sit on the bridge of his narrow nose over deep-set hazel eyes. His thin lips are bent in the shape of a humorless smile.

That sensation of familiarity crashes into me like a violent ocean wave. I know this older version of the man. I know him well. I try to remember and the terror rises, convulsing, and overwhelms me. I reluctantly back down.

"Holy shit," Mike breathes. "That's – that's Reid Reddick."

"Yes, except according to this website his name is Daniel Maines."

Mike sits back in his chair, thunderstruck. It takes him a long time to find his words. "That son of a bitch stole his million-dollar client's dead son's identity."

"Yep, and he did it to avoid getting caught for stealing other clients' money," Nic says.

Mike tosses his pen onto his desk. "There's a special place in hell for assholes like this." He takes a couple beats to pull himself together, then asks, "Do we have the real Daniel Maines' Social Security number?"

Nic takes his computer back and starts typing. "No. I'll ask Jodi if she can provide."

"Do that. If she can, run it through Minnesota's public records databases."

"Cora can help me with that." Nic says, nodding.

"And keep me posted."

Nic says he will and heads back out to the bullpen. Mike sits for a moment, staring at the far wall. "I'll be goddamned," he murmurs, then shakes it off and returns to his work. He pauses briefly to say one thing to Cardinal Doe's sketch: "We're getting close, kiddo. I can feel it."

He's in the middle of composing a lengthy email, hunting and pecking the keyboard with only his two pointer fingers, when his desk phone rings. He reaches over and opens the line on speaker without looking away from his screen. "Franklin."

"Hi Mike." Now there's a voice I haven't heard in a while. It's a little raspier, but still high-pitched and sing-songy. Someone else is on the crime beat for KDJR now, has been for years, so Mike hasn't interacted with this particular reporter in a long time.

Mike's chin drops to his chest with a sigh. "Kristina."

"How you holding up these days?"

"Fine, thanks. How can I help you?" His voice is carefully neutral.

"I don't know if you heard, but I'm the lifestyle reporter for the morning show now, and I was thinking about the fundraiser your team did recently for your Cardinal Doe."

"What about it?" Mike's tone is a little bit friendlier, but still laced with suspicion.

"Well, I'm sure you know that my segment really helped get your fundraiser over the finish line."

"Nic did mention that," Mike concedes.

"Oh, that Dominic is a real peach, Mike. Hang on to him."

"I plan to." He tries to suppress a small smile.

"Anyway, we've had hundreds of people call in since then looking for an update, and I'd love to do a followup. People remember her, you know?"

Mike squeezes his eyes shut. "I know."

"So what do you say?"

Mike ponders. "I don't have any material updates to share right now, but I can say that we're making progress. I'll tell you what. If and when we bring this case to a resolution, you will be the first to know."

Kristina's breath catches in her throat, like she'd been steeling herself for another angry outburst and was surprised by his response. I'll be honest, it surprised me too. "Really?"

"Yeah. I owe you one for being such a colossal asshole the first time around."

Silence from the other end.

"Kristina? Still there?"

"I'm here. I—ah, I know I pushed you too hard. I'm as much of an asshole here as you are. Are we good?"

Mike smiles. "We're good. Thanks for the call, Kristina. We'll talk soon."

"Bye, Mike."

Mike ends the call and goes back to his email. Nothing's physically changed, yet he seems…lighter somehow. Like he's been relieved of a burden he didn't realize he was carrying.

I think he's getting his first taste of forgiveness.

CHAPTER 16

Mike has just finished saying his usual hello to Cardinal Doe's charm bracelet when Nic appears at his door holding a sheaf of printed papers. "Holy shit, boss."

Mike chuckles. "Good morning to you too, Detective. Come on in."

Nic's blue eyes dance. "Cora just faxed over everything she was able to find about Daniel Maines."

"All right, lay it on me." Mike takes a big gulp of coffee from a Minnesota Vikings mug that has definitely seen better days, then picks up his pen and starts clicking.

Nic reads from his printouts. "According to this, Daniel Alton Maines, date of birth July 27, 1955, has no criminal history. Just two speeding tickets and a couple of civil actions related to his business. He's held a valid Minnesota driver's license since June of 1991. He married Kimberly Pettit in September 1991. Their first daughter, Samantha Louise Maines, was born in December of that same year."

Samantha Louise Maines. The name hits me like a bomb, obliterating everything. The terror and the pain that isolated me from my memories for so long dissolve like smoke. Samantha Maines. That's my name. That's *me.* Daniel Maines is my father, and Kimberly Maines is my mother. I remember them. I *know* them.

Holy shit.

Nic is still talking. "He built his house in Caribou Creek, Minnesota, in 1992. His second daughter, Schuyler Belle Maines, was born in March 1993."

At the mention of my sister's name, an invisible dam lets go and memories start flooding back. So many memories. Birthday parties. Walking barefoot on the muddy banks of Caribou Creek, hunting for crawdads and frogs. Riding our bikes to the convenience store and blowing all our allowance money on candy. Painting each other's nails. Fighting over clothes. All the things sisters do, Sky and I did. She was my built-in best friend. How could I forget I had a sister?

"Foundations Wealth Advisors registered with the state of Minnesota as a limited liability company in August 1995." Nic pauses to take one final breath, then says, "And Daniel Maines has paid his income taxes faithfully every year since 1992."

"Reid Reddick disappeared when?" Mike asks.

"May 25, 1991." Nic recites the date from memory.

More silence while Mike absorbs this. "Is there anything on that Social Security number before June of 1991?"

Nic looks at his papers. "Ah, let's see." He runs his finger down a column of dense text. "The last hit before that was when he was hired at Whelan Manufacturing in south Minneapolis in April of 1987."

"That would have been the real Daniel Maines," Mike says.

"Right."

"So there's nothing between April 1987 and June 1991."

"Correct."

"What is the real Daniel Maines' date of death?"

Nic consults his notes. "He died on October 22, 1989. He was only thirty-four years old."

Mike is quiet for a long time. Then: "So not only did Reid Reddick steal a dead man's identity, he abandoned his family and used that identity to start a new life and a new family."

Nic gives a heavy sigh. "I mean…yeah. That's what it looks like." Suddenly he perks up a bit. "Wait. Do you think one of the daughters could be Cardinal Doe?"

Yes! I try to shout. *It's me! I'm Samantha!*

Mike suddenly shudders and runs his hands over his arms. "Is it cold in here? Or is it just me?"

Nic shrugs. "I think it's actually sort of warm in here."

"Huh." Mike shakes his head. "Where was I? Oh. There's no way any of this is a coincidence. Run these people down and see what you turn up."

Nic leaves and Mike props his elbows on his desk and rests his head in his hands. I suspect he's beating himself up over all the things he thinks he should have done differently with my case.

"You all right, boss?" Eric Plummer is standing at the door, concern swirling in his deep black eyes.

Mike sits up straight. "Come on in, E. I'm fi–" Mike stops himself and sighs. "You know what, it's pointless to lie. I – ah, I've been having kind of a rough time lately. The Cardinal Doe case is taking a lot out of me. But I will be okay. I recently started talking to someone."

Eric sits in the chair Nic recently vacated. "I'm glad to hear it. Is it helping?"

"I've only had a couple of sessions, but I'm hopeful."

Eric extends his fist across the desk, and Mike bumps it with his own, almost like they're toasting with beer steins. "Proud of you, boss. I know it isn't easy to admit when you need help."

Mike sighs again. "Thanks. Enough about me, now. What do you got?"

"Nothing, boss. Saw you sitting at your desk holding your head, wanted to make sure everything's all right."

Mike nods. "I appreciate that, E. Thank you."

"No problem." Eric slowly stands and lumbers out the door, leaving Mike to think about the latest twist in the Cardinal Doe case.

I have plenty to think about, myself.

CHAPTER 17

I always figured I had memories of my life and my death hiding somewhere behind that ever-threatening avalanche of terror and pain. I mean, who becomes aware of their own existence only after they've died? That doesn't make any sense. All the time I've been with Mike, I learned to focus on the now, and be okay with knowing nothing about who I really am and what happened to me.

That's all changed now that I know my name: Samantha Louise Maines. The fear is gone, dissipated like a summer morning fog. Memories wash over me like an entirely different tsunami.

I remember my family. My dad, Daniel, spent most of his time working. He wasn't an attentive father and left the task of raising my sister and me to our mom. He missed out on basically all of our milestones and achievements. When he was around, he was controlling and demanding and kind of mean. One time, when I was in middle school, I made the mistake of telling him I had other plans when he wanted Sky and me to spend a beautiful fall Saturday doing chores.

∞

I'm startled awake when my dad noisily opens my bedroom door and flips on the light. "Get up," he growls, then does the same thing to Sky.

I groan and pull my comforter over my head to block the light. "It's Saturday!"

"The yard needs to be raked," he says, with no sympathy or understanding at all. "You two get your asses moving."

I don't want to rake the yard. It's huge and completely covered in leaves. It'll take hours, even with Sky's help. I don't have hours. Marley's birthday party is today, and I can't miss it. I won't. Ever since she found out she has leukemia, she's been sad and depressed and sick from the chemo, and she needs this party to cheer her up. Not even the Jonas Brothers could keep me away.

I roll out of bed and stand in my bedroom doorway. The oversized t-shirt I slept in hangs to my knees. "I can't rake the yard today, Dad, I have a party to go to. Marley's party."

My dad, who had been walking away, stops and slowly turns to face me. A deep crease appears between his eyebrows. "Excuse me?"

"Sami!" Sky is standing in her doorway too, right next to me. Her hair is rumpled and her eyes are round, like a cartoon character's. "Don't make him mad," she whispers.

Screw that. This is my best friend we're talking about. "I'll rake tomorrow."

"Our house looks like the neighborhood hoarder house. It's embarrassing. I want it done today."

I cross my arms, partly in defiance, and partly to hide the wild jackrabbiting of my heart. I'm scared, but I refuse to back down. "I'm not doing it today."

My dad crosses the space between us like he's wearing Hermes' winged shoes. We just finished a Greek Mythology unit in my English class, so I know all about Hermes and how he guided souls to the afterlife. The rage in my dad's eyes makes me wonder if Hermes will be coming for me next. He grabs me tightly and digs his fingertips hard into the sensitive skin of my underarm. It hurts, but I refuse to show it.

"You little brat," he hisses. Tiny drops of spit hit my face. Gross. "I work my ass off to put a roof over your head and food on the table, and pay for your clothes and your sports, and this is how you thank me? You should be kissing my fucking feet."

I look him dead in the eye, but don't say anything. This enrages him more, but he lets go of my arm with a little push. "Get out," he snarls. "You want to go to the Richters' so bad? Pack a bag and go. And don't come back."

"No!" Sky wails.

He turns on her. "You want to go with her?"

Sky shakes her head and tries to make herself smaller. "No, Daddy."

"Then shut up." He turns his attention back to me. "You're still standing here? Get the fuck out of my house."

My heart races and tears prickle behind my eyes, but I keep my face still. My dad lunges a little as if he's going to come after me and inflict some real damage, but he ends up just stomping upstairs and out of the house. His car starts up and the tires screech a little as he roars away.

Sky is devastated. "Why did you do that, Sami? He's kicking you out! And now I have to do the yard all by myself!"

I hug her. "All I did was not let him push me around. I won't be gone long. I promise."

I pack a bag, hug Sky again, and leave the house. The crisp fall morning makes the two-mile walk to Marley's house bearable. I know Steph Richter will pull Marley's trundle bed out and let me stay however long it takes for *my mom to call, looking for me. This isn't the first time we've been through this rodeo.*

And it won't be the last.

∞

While life with my narcissist father was difficult, life with my warm and caring mother, Kimberly, was mostly good. She worked as a personal trainer and did her best to offset my dad's unpredictable swings. It was hard, and she abused alcohol, specifically red wine, to cope. There were many times my sister or I would find her passed out sitting on the couch, wine glass tipping precariously to the side in her limp hand. Sometimes we got to her in time to stop it from spilling, and sometimes we didn't. Now I realize that's probably why I'm so concerned about Mike and his alcohol problem.

My sister Schuyler, Sky for short, was my Irish twin. Only fifteen months separated us in age, and we looked enough alike with our brown eyes and long curly brown hair that we were usually mistaken for actual twins. We got our gorgeous hair from our mother, and she always said we got our smart mouths from our father.

We lived in Caribou Creek, Minnesota, an old Mississippi River town about thirty miles northwest of Minneapolis. I ran cross country and track at Caribou Creek High School (go Reindeer!), and Marley was my best friend for life. I remember her bright red hair, her obnoxiously loud laugh, her obsession with country music, and her amazing ability to listen and empathize.

I think if I tried hard enough, I might be able to remember the circumstances of my death. But you know what? I don't think I want to know that yet. I would much rather enjoy the positive vibes of the happy memories right now. I waited long enough for them. The rest will come soon enough, I'm sure.

I miss my mom. I miss my sister. I hope they're okay. Do they ever think about me?

Do they miss me, too?

CHAPTER 18

When Mike arrives and pulls out his recorder, he surprises me with what he has to say.

"Mike Franklin, checking in. Today's date is Thursday, September fourth, oh-eight-hundred hours. I had another dream last night."

I brace myself for a new, awful nightmare.

"I'm walking down my street. It's a beautiful summer evening. It's sunny, neighbors are out mowing their lawns or grilling, kids are playing basketball in their driveways. Everyone stops what they're doing and waves hello as I walk by. I wave back.

"One house is watering their lawn with one of those pulsating sprinklers. Every time the sprinkler spins back to its starting position, the water hits the leaves of an ash tree next to the street. A bright red cardinal is sitting on the lowest branch of that tree, chirping and fluffing out its feathers and just enjoying its evening bath." He pauses. "It would shake the water off, then do it all again. I've never seen such a happy little bird."

I think of Bella and Edward, my cardinal friends in the forest. They brought me so much joy during those early days, as I waited forever for my remains to be found. They're long gone now, but hopefully their descendants are still there, building nests and tending to their babies.

Mike pauses again and reaches for the bracelet. "Cardinals appear when angels are near," he murmurs. Then he picks up the photo of Rachel and Kylie. "Did my angels visit me last night?" His voice cracks on that last word, and he takes a deep breath to steady himself.

Just in time, too. There's a knock at his door. He quickly sets the photo aside and clears his throat. "Yeah. Come in."

It's Nic. "Boss. You are not going to believe what I've got on our girl."

Mike points to the chair. "Sit. Speak."

Nic sits. "I did like you said and did some digging on our friend Reid Reddick-slash-Daniel Maines. And…well, holy shit."

Mike's eyebrows hit his hairline.

"I called the Caribou Creek, Minnesota police department and asked the lady who answered the phone if they were familiar with a resident named Daniel Maines. She didn't say anything for so long that I thought I'd lost the connection. Then she said 'Hold on,' and put me through to Detective James Gardiner. He's kind of a churlish fellow."

Mike says what I'm thinking. "'Churlish?' What are you, a dictionary?"

Nic grins. "Gardiner's been around a long time. I gotta imagine he's counting down the days until retirement."

Mike nods. "Too many years in this job can break a man's spirit, if he's not careful." Mike would know. "What did Detective Gardiner have to say about Daniel Maines?"

Nic opens his laptop and pulls up his notes. "Daniel and Kimberly Maines lead a pretty quiet life. They have had only one law enforcement call to their house, and that was the day their oldest daughter went missing."

Mike suddenly, violently sits up straight in his chair, then stands, plants his hands on the desk, and leans closer to Nic. His eyes are dinner plates. "WHAT?"

His bellow causes some unrest in the bullpen outside his open door. Jewel pokes her head in. "Everything okay in here?"

Mike waves her away. "Fine, fine."

"All right." Jewel raises her hands and backs out of the doorway. "He says everything's fine." Her voice is low but still perfectly audible. I'm sure the whole team is hanging out there now, listening. As I am. Closely.

"I know, right? I was as shocked as you are," Nic says.

"What's the story?" Mike recovers his composure enough to sit back down, then picks up his pen and starts clicking it vigorously.

"According to Gardiner, sixteen-year-old Samantha Maines went for her morning run on the twenty-sixth of July, 2008. She usually did her runs in a nearby park called Forest Trails. She never came home and hasn't been seen or heard from since."

Mike says nothing, just stares at Nic and clicks his pen.

"Samantha was a pretty typical suburban teenager: pretty, popular, a good student, a standout runner. Well-regarded by her classmates, teachers, and coaches. She was going to be a junior at Caribou Creek High School in the fall."

"What did Detective Gardiner do to try and find her?" Mike asks.

"It's the goddamndest thing, boss. Caribou Creek treated Samantha's disappearance exactly the same way Minneapolis did Reid Reddick's. They didn't do a damn thing except take a missing person report and post her photo to social media." Nic shakes his head. "Actually, that's not the whole truth. They did also get her out on missing person databases, and they shared her photo with patrol so they could keep an eye out for her. But that's it. No searches, no nothing. Because, and I quote, 'Teenagers are considered runaways unless there's evidence of foul play.'"

"Jesus Christ, what is it with these police departments in the Twin Cities?" Mike asks, incredulous. *Click-click-click.*

"I didn't say anything, but sometimes my face speaks for me," Nic says with a grimace. "Gardiner got kind of defensive. Swears he pushed to investigate Samantha's disappearance, but was shot down by the brass. Caribou Creek has changed their policy since then, and now they investigate all missing person reports."

"Great." Sarcasm dripped from that single word like molasses.

"I told Gardiner that I'm investigating a Jane Doe and that I need to speak with Daniel Maines and his family. He asked about that, and I filled him in on our girl. I also told him about our suspicions that Daniel Maines is not who he says he is. 'I always knew that fucker was crooked,' he said. Well, it was more of a growl, but you catch my drift. Then he asked if he could help. I think he really does feel bad about not doing more back in '08."

"How old did you say Samantha was when she went missing?" *Click-click-click.*

Nic double-checks his notes. "Sixteen."

"M.E. said Cardinal Doe was likely between eighteen and twenty-four," Mike points out.

"I looked into that," Nic says. "He noted in the autopsy report that his estimated age range was mostly based on the fact that all four of Cardinal Doe's wisdom teeth had fully grown in. That's fairly rare for people younger than seventeen or eighteen."

Mike's pen abruptly stops clicking. "Samantha Maines is our Cardinal Doe," he says simply.

Finally. I wish I could hug him.

Nic nods. "I think so, too."

"We need to get DNA from the entire Maines family," Mike says. "That's how we're going to prove it. Once we officially ID her, we'll work with Caribou Creek to figure out how in the hell she ended up dead in Superior, Wisconsin."

"Permission to go back to the Twin Cities?" Nic asks with a grin.

"Permission granted. Get out of here and go make shit happen."

"On it, boss." Nic walks out the door and says, "Oh, hey guys. Enjoying the show?"

I knew it. They were all out there, listening. The party breaks up and they all go back to their desks.

Mike picks up the Cardinal Doe sketch and gazes at it for a long time. "Samantha Maines," he says, his voice low. "Is that your name?"

Yes. That's my name.

Mike gets up and closes his office door, then sits and reaches for his desk phone. He dials, waits a few seconds, then says, "Hello, this is Michael Franklin. Is Dr. Atkinson available? Thank you." He waits a few more seconds, then says, "Hey, Jackie, how are you?" He pauses, listening. "I'm not going to lie, I'm feeling kind of rough this morning." Pause. "Yeah, it's the Cardinal Doe case. Nic made a breakthrough and now we think we know who she is. The thing is, I should be happy about that. Ecstatic. Over the goddamn moon. But I'm not. I feel like an absolute failure. Again. I don't know what's wrong with me." He listens for quite a while, then says: "Yeah, you've said that before and it makes complete sense. It does. I just can't seem to let go of the fact that Nic is doing this now because I failed to do it back in '09." A pause. "That's true, I was in a very bad place back then, dealing with the loss of my wife and daughter. That's no excuse. I should have tried harder. A good detective never gives up." Pause. "Yes, of course I've heard the term 'trauma response.'" Longer pause. "No, I've never been officially diagnosed with post-traumatic stress disorder." A much longer pause, and realization suddenly dawns in Mike's eyes. "Wait. So you're saying that my…all right, we'll call it what it is, my *obsession* with Cardinal Doe is a trauma response to my wife's postpartum psychotic break?" Mike's eyes widen as he absorbs this. "I mean, no. That has never occurred to me. I just figured it was my first case as a detective and —" Pause. "Ah, I'd really rather not say." Another pause. "Well, because if my Chief finds out, I'm likely out of a job. For now just understand that I think about having a drink every second of every day." Pause. "The drinking is also a trauma response. I think I'm beginning to see a pattern here." Long pause. "Yes, I think so, too. Thank you, Jackie. This was really helpful and I like the idea of making some changes to my therapy plan. I'll see you at our regularly scheduled time on Wednesday. Buh-bye." Mike hangs up the phone and sits back in his chair, then spends a good amount of time staring at the wall behind his desk. "Huh. I guess that explains the dreams," he says, making me wonder, again, if he somehow feels me here.

He picks up the photo of his family and gazes at it for a while, then says, "I think I know now what I need to do, babe.

"I finally understand the assignment."

CHAPTER 19

I know it's Wednesday because Mike is gone for a good chunk of the morning. He's seeing Dr. Atkinson and hopefully making some progress on his therapy plan.

When he walks into his office, he looks a little better. Rested. He's even smiling at something Simon said as he walked through the bullpen. Nic is right behind him.

"I assume you've met with the Maines family?" Mike sets his bag down on his desk.

"Yeah, Jim Gardiner and I met with them at the Caribou Creek PD."

"How did that go?" Mike is sitting in his chair now, pen in hand, thumb ready to start clicking.

"We separated them right away – Daniel in one room, Kimberly and Schuyler in another. We let Daniel simmer while we talked with his wife and daughter. Jim had one of his colleagues keep an eye on the room's camera for us. Maines was nervous, and the long wait only made him sweat more."

"Good." *Click-click-click.*

"After talking to Kimberly and Schuyler, Jim and I are satisfied that they didn't have anything to do with Samantha's disappearance. Kimberly said she had an early training appointment with a longstanding client that morning. Samantha was home when she left."

I was, in fact, still in bed, trying to talk myself out of running and sleep in instead. I couldn't do it. Cross country season was due to start in August, just a couple weeks away, and I needed to be in tip-top shape. Skipping a run was out of the question.

I'm starting to remember.

"Schuyler was at work as well," Nic says. "She'd just started working at one of those fast food joints. Samantha actually dropped her off there before heading to the park for her run."

That's right. I did.

∞

The sun is out, there's a slight breeze, and the humidity isn't too bad. It's a perfect day for a nice long run at Forest Trails Park. If Sky can ever get her shit together and come out to the car.

I honk and roll my window down. "Sky! Let's go! You're going to be late!"

"I'm coming!" She's tying her apron strings behind her back as she walks quickly out of the garage. She has a matching hat in her hand. She gets in the car and fastens her seat belt.

"You look like a dork in fast food fashion." My charm bracelet clinks on my arm as I slide my sunglasses on my nose. "Brown is not your color."

Sky shoots me a death glare. "Please stop wearing your hair in a ponytail and use it to cover your face. You scare the children." She crosses her arms and stares straight ahead.

I burst out laughing. She can't hide a smile, either.

Houses and trees whiz by as I drive out of the neighborhood. "Are you excited?" I ask. Today's only her second day at her new job, and the first day she'll be doing actual work instead of orientation stuff.

"Yeah. I just hope I don't mess anything up."

"You will," I said. "But that's okay. You're learning. The trick is to not be too hard on yourself about it. Everyone makes mistakes." I know she will be hard on herself because our dad conditioned her to be. Nothing she does is ever quite good enough for him, and she wants his approval more than anything. Me? I don't need it. Good thing, too, because his love and approval always come with strings attached.

Sky sighs. "Just watch. I'll be the first trainee in history to burn a restaurant down because I don't know how to work the deep fryer."

"If that happened, it would be their fault for expecting you to know that on day two." I give her a reassuring smile and squeeze her knee. "You're going to do great. I know it."

She tries to smile. "Thanks."

We chit-chat about mundane things like friends and school until we get to the restaurant. I turn into the parking lot and pull right up to the door. "Front door service," I announce.

"Thanks for the ride." Then she does something I don't expect: she leans over and plants a kiss on my cheek. "Love you, sis. Be safe."

My hand flies to my face. She doesn't wait for me to find the words to tell her I love her too. She gets out of the car and goes inside, emboldened and ready to take on her second day.

God, I love that kid.

∞

My heart is heavy. I didn't know that would be the last time I would see my sister.

Nic continues. "Jim and I asked Kimberly and Schuyler to wait, and then we went next door to have a chat with Daniel Maines."

"How did that go?" *Click-click-click.*

"Let's just say that Daniel Maines, Reid Reddick, whatever the hell his name is, is an unpleasant individual. I see what his first wife Susan means when she says he was a self-absorbed and neglectful husband and father. I think he's a card-carrying narcissist."

"What did he have to say?" Mike asks, his pen still clicking rapidly.

"He swears he was at home all day when Samantha went missing and he never saw her, but – I don't know, boss, there was something in his eyes that made me think he doesn't actually remember that day. I don't know if it's because he doesn't care and can't be bothered, or if he legit can't remember. I mean, whether he's Daniel Maines, who would be sixty-nine this year, or Reid Reddick, who is –" Nic consults his notes "– almost seventy-four years old now, he's no spring chicken. Maybe he has actual memory problems."

"No. There's no way in hell a father forgets the day his kid went missing." Mike's eyes are ablaze, and I know he's thinking about his own kid. He'll remember the day she died in excruciating detail for the rest of his life.

"Okay, then we'll go with can't be bothered and doesn't care," Nic says. "That fits his personality, or lack thereof, much better anyway. He blamed the Caribou Creek PD for not finding Samantha. Said if they'd done their fucking jobs, she'd have come home a long time ago. Oh boy, did that raise Jim Gardiner's hackles. I thought he was going to come across the table and throttle Reddick. Maines. Whatever we're calling him."

"I mean, he's not wrong," Mike points out.

"True. But Gardiner made a solid point when he asked Maines what all he did to look for his daughter over the years. You know what that fucker said? 'That's your fucking job, not mine.'"

Mike's mouth drops open. "Holy shit."

"Right?" Nic scrolls through his notes. "I decided it was time to cut to the chase. I told him I'm doing *my* fucking job. Then I pulled out a photo of Cardinal Doe's charm bracelet and set it on the table in front of him. All he could do was just stare at it. His face turned white, like paper-white. I thought for a second he might pass out."

"Did he say anything?" Mike asks, rapt.

"Yeah, he said it's Samantha's bracelet, she got it from her best friend who died like a year before Samantha went missing. She never took it off."

Another memory crashes over me, this one of the worst day of my life. Well, the second-worst day, I guess.

∞

Marley Richter is my best friend, and she's dying. I've been by her side since she was diagnosed with acute lymphocytic leukemia in the eighth grade. I consoled her when she lost her gorgeous red hair to chemotherapy. I made her eat when she started losing alarming amounts of weight — even when she didn't want to. We watched movies and played video games. On the days when she felt weak, I carried her books to class. When she stopped going to school, I went to her house every day and brought her homework. It's been a lot for a teenage girl to handle, but I never thought twice about it. I knew she would do the same for me if roles were reversed.

She'd been fighting this awful disease for over a year when two months ago the doctors told her mom there was nothing more they could do for her. She started receiving hospice care at home, and that was the beginning of the end. We've watched her just waste away. Her skin, once a perfect shade of ivory, is now a scary gray color, and she is so thin. Almost skeletal.

It's spring break from school when the phone rings at my house at six o'clock in the morning, waking me up. I lay in my bed and listen as my mom answers it.

"Hello? Oh, Steph, hi. How are you?" Pause. "Oh. Oh, no, is she—" Pause. "I understand. I'm so, so sorry."

I jump out of bed and run to my mother. She's sitting on the couch in her morning robe, the cordless phone pressed to her ear. Her eyes are wide. I sit next to her and wait for what I know will be bad news.

"Yes, of course I'll tell her. Will you let me know if there's anything I can do? Okay. Okay, bye." She turns the phone off and lets it fall to her lap.

"What happened?" I whisper. My heart is pounding so hard it makes my voice shake.

"Um. Marley had a seizure last night. She's at the hospital now, and it's pretty touch and go." My mother looks at me with shiny eyes. "She wants to see you."

"Then let's go." I hop off the couch and head for my room to change.

"Sami."

I stop. I know that tone. I whirl around and go on the offense. "Don't bother saying it, Mom. I'm going."

"I don't think it's a good idea. Is this how you want to remember her? Wouldn't you rather remember her as she was when she was healthy?"

"Let me put it this way. If you don't drive me to the hospital right now, I will walk there."

"Sami, the hospital is fifteen miles away."

"Then I'll run there." My voice is shaking again, this time from the herculean effort it's taking to not scream at her.

She raises her hands in front of her. "Fine, fine."

I quickly change and throw my hair up in a messy bun, and away we go. Adrenaline and cortisol flood my veins, and I cannot stop fidgeting. How bad is she? Will she still be alive when I get there? What if I don't get the chance to say goodbye? This thought brings tears to my eyes.

"Hurry up."

"Sami, I'm going as fast as I dare."

We finally get to the hospital and Mom pulls up in front of the main entrance. "I'll see—"

The slam of the car door cuts her off, and I start running. I skip the elevators and run up the stairs. My panicked footfalls echo in the cavernous open stairwell. When I finally get to the fifth floor pediatric ward, I burst through the door, sweating and panting. The nurses at the main station stop what they're doing and turn to look at me. "M-Marley? Marley Richter?"

"Are you Samantha?" A younger nurse with kind eyes asks.

I don't think I can say any more words without breaking down, so I simply nod.

She points down the hallway to my right. "She's in room five-oh-seven."

I nod again, still mute, and slowly make my way down the hall. I try to ignore the stench of urine and antiseptic. The fluorescent lights seem way too bright. Tears prickle behind my eyes; I am absolutely terrified of what I'm going to see when I walk into her room.

Marley's mom, Steph, sees me standing uncertainly at the door of her darkened room and comes to me. Marley got her ivory skin and red hair from her mother, and sometimes I look at Steph and recall how Marley looked when she was healthy. Now, though, Steph looks awful. She's been crying a lot and sleeping very little. "Oh, thank god you're here, Sami." She wraps me in a big hug, and my own tears start to fall.

"Is she okay?" I sob.

Steph lets me go and wipes her eyes as she looks toward the bed. It's covered with Marley's favorite green fleece blanket. She's hooked up to numerous machines and a fat IV bag. I can barely see the top of the green knit cap covering her head. "I think this is it, baby. The doctors don't think she'll last much longer." She keeps her voice low so Marley can't hear her.

I go to my friend. She looks tiny and so frail, curled up in the fetal position. She's gotten a lot worse since I last saw her a couple days ago. I think Steph's right; Marley won't be going home. Fresh tears flood my eyes. "Mar?"

Her eyes flutter open. "Sami?" Her voice even sounds frail.

I sit in the chair next to the bed so my face is even with hers. I carefully wrap one of her cold, bony hands in mine. "I'm here." I can't stop the tears, so I just let them fall.

"You came," she whispers.

"Of course I came."

"I…have something…for you." Even the simple act of speaking a few words is draining what little precious energy she has. "My mom…"

"I have it right here, baby." Steph hands me a small, flat box.

I gently disentangle my hand from Marley's and take it. "What is this?"

"It's…a gift…to remember me."

I wipe my whole wet face with the bottom of my t-shirt, then open the box. A silver charm bracelet lay on a cotton pad inside. I carefully lift it up and examine it. "Oh, Mar, it's perfect." I read the inscription on the back of the cardinal charm and burst into fresh tears.

"I'll…always…be with…you," Marley whispers.

I lean over her and give her the best hug I can without disturbing her lifelines or crushing her fragile body. "Thank you," I sob. "I'll wear it forever."

"I…love you…Sami."

I slide the bracelet onto my right wrist; it jingles as I take her hand again. "I love you too, Mar."

Marley closes her eyes. Steph climbs into bed with her and holds her tight. My mom comes up behind me and lays a warm, comforting hand on my shoulder. We all cry silently as we listen to her shallow, slowing breaths. I know she's taken her last when the machines around us start beeping stridently. Nurses rush in, followed by a doctor who is sticking his stethoscope in his ears as he runs. My mom gently pulls me away from Marley to make room for them.

"No!" I sob. "Marley! No!"

Steph stumbles over to us and we stand near the door with our arms around each other. The medical team doesn't try to resuscitate her. They would probably break her if they did. Instead they check her vitals and the doctor looks at his watch. "Time of death, eight-oh-four A.M."

My best friend is gone. My heart is broken.

Steph's wails gut me even more. It's the tortured sound of a single mom losing her only child after fighting like hell to save her.

The doctor goes to her and takes her hands. His eyes are sad. "I'm sorry, Steph. I'm so sorry."

Just as the doctor leaves, Marley's grandparents, Steph's parents, arrive. "Are we too late?" her grandma shouts. "Oh my god, are we too late?"

My mom decides this is the right time for us to leave. She guides me out the door and through the labyrinthian maze of hallways and elevators until we finally reach the car. I've stopped crying, at least for the moment. Now I'm just numb. I don't know what life will be like without my best friend around. I don't want to know.

What I do know is, I will miss her for the rest of my life.

∞

The memory shatters my heart again. If I were able to cry, I would make it rain for my Mar.

"What else did Maines say when he saw the bracelet?" Mike asks.

"He asked what happened to her. I told him all I know is this bracelet was on human remains that were found in Superior, Wisconsin in April of 2009. I told him I need to positively identify those remains, and I need his DNA to do it. Maines closed up like a trap and said, 'I'm not giving you my fucking DNA.' That's when Jim excused himself and he took the photo of the bracelet with him. He was gone for like twenty minutes. I kept trying to get Maines to talk, but he wouldn't respond to any of my questions."

"Did you confront him about his real identity?" Mike asks.

"I was tempted, but I want to keep that close to the vest until we have DNA."

"Makes sense."

Nic continues. "When Jim came back, he was carrying two DNA collection kits and told Daniel he got what we needed from his wife and daughter. The man went ballistic. Shouted something about privacy and how fucking dare we and he'll sue us and our departments into oblivion. I asked him, I said, 'What's the problem, Daniel? Don't you want to know if our Jane Doe is your missing daughter?' Maines folded his arms over his chest and refused to speak again. He looked like a preschooler stuck in an old man's body."

That sounds like my dad. He always had to have his way. And he usually got it. But on the rare occasion he didn't, he behaved like a petulant child. He was always sort of an enigma. Not particularly warm or empathetic, not generous with love or acceptance, sometimes mean for sport. His temper was the stuff of legend. I tried to love him, but I didn't dare love him too loudly. Mostly I just tried to stay out of his way.

"Given his reaction when he found out we got DNA from Kimberly and Schuyler, I think it's a pretty safe bet that Daniel Maines is indeed Reid Reddick," Nic says.

"We'll find out soon enough." Mike tosses his pen on his desk. "Once you get those DNA kits over to Michelle Musgrove."

"Jim couriered them over while I was still in Caribou Creek. She already has them."

"Beautiful," Mike says. Then: "I'd like to take a look at Caribou Creek's files on Samantha Maines. Do you have a copy?"

The printer outside Mike's office is already spitting out paper. Nic retrieves the printouts and hands them to Mike. The sheaf of papers is pathetically thin. "Naturally."

"Thanks." Mike slides his glasses on his nose.

"Anytime," Nic says as he gathers up his things and heads for the door.

"Oh, hey, Nic?" Mike calls after him.

"Yeah, boss?"

A genuine smile crosses Mike's face, crinkling his cheeks and the corners of his eyes. "Nice work."

Nic's ears turn pink and he dips his head, then disappears.

Mike turns his attention to the Samantha Maines file. "We're almost there, kiddo," he murmurs.

"We're almost there."

CHAPTER 20

Mike walks into his office holding a bag from Stewie's, his favorite sandwich shop. Inside I know there's a pastrami on rye with swiss cheese and lots of mustard, wrapped in waxed paper. And if Cornelia is working today, there's probably a chocolate chip cookie in there too, "an extra treat for my favorite police officer." His sunglasses are perched on top of his head.

Nic walks in right behind him. "Hey, boss."

Mike sits at his desk and pulls his sandwich out of the bag. "Can it wait, Morris? I'm about to put this delicious Stewie's sandwich directly into my belly."

Nic shrugs. "I mean, sure, it can wait." He turns for the door. "I just thought you'd like to know that DNA came back on Cardinal Doe." He takes a couple steps as if he's going to leave, trying to suppress a smirk.

"Hold it." Mike suddenly loses all interest in his sandwich, halfway through unwrapping it. "What does it say?"

Nic grins and sits in his usual chair. "It confirms what we basically already knew. Michelle says that Kimberly Maines' DNA confirms with one hundred percent confidence that Cardinal Doe is her biological daughter. Schuyler's DNA confirms that she is Cardinal Doe's sister; they both share roughly fifty percent of their DNA with Kimberly. Given that, there's only one person who could be our Cardinal Doe."

"Samantha Maines," Mike says.

"You got it. But wait, there's more. I asked Michelle to compare the Maines women's DNA to Victoria Reddick's. Schuyler shares roughly the same amount of DNA with Tori that Samantha does – twenty-six percent. Tori doesn't share any DNA with Kimberly. You know what that means?"

"I'm going to guess that means it's highly likely that Victoria is Samantha and Schuyler's half-sister, and they have the same father. Reid Reddick."

"Michelle won't officially say that without his DNA, but she admits it seems to be the most likely scenario."

"I guess that's as close as we're going to get to proving Reid Reddick is Daniel Maines until he surrenders his DNA." Mike rubs his hand over the lower half of his face, thinking. Then he says, "I'd like Michelle to run one more test for us. I don't know where we are with her retainer, but I will find the money if we need it."

"Okay," Nic says.

"Have her test the spot of blood on Cardi–I mean, Samantha's shirt."

Nic stands. "On it. I'll call Gardiner too and give him the news. He can notify the family. And maybe he can talk Maines into giving up his DNA."

"Sounds like a plan," Mike says. "Now get the hell out, I have a sandwich to devour."

Nic leaves, laughing.

Mike chuckles as he finishes unwrapping his sandwich. It's a genuine chuckle, full of good humor. The heavy emotional weight he's carried all these years seems to have lifted a little bit more with the official confirmation of Cardinal Doe's identity. I don't think he's jealous or feels like a failure anymore.

I think he's finally beginning to see the light at the end of the long, dark tunnel he's been in for so many years.

CHAPTER 21

Mike has his glasses on and is reading emails when Nic appears at his door and knocks. "Hey, boss."

Mike doesn't turn around. "Hey, Nic."

"Can you spare a few minutes for a video call with Michelle Musgrove? She's got an update for us."

This catches Mike's attention; he turns and looks up at Nic over the top of his glasses. "Sure. Here?"

"Yeah." Nic sits and positions his laptop so both detectives are visible on the screen. He clicks a couple of things and before long Michelle's face appears.

"Hello," she says.

Mike picks up his pen and gets right to the point. "What do you got for us, Michelle?"

"Well, Nic asked if I could test the spot of blood that was found on Cardinal Doe's shirt. I was able to develop a full DNA profile, and then I compared it to the profiles of Kimberly Maines, Schuyler Maines, and Victoria Reddick. I found that the person who left that blood on Cardinal Doe—"

"Samantha," Mike corrects her.

"Right, yes, Samantha Maines. The person who left the blood on her shirt is Victoria's full brother, likely Schuyler's half-brother, and has no shared DNA with Kimberly Maines."

Nic and Mike stare at each other, thunderstruck. Nic places his hands on his head, elbows sticking out to the sides, and his eyes are wide. "Holy shit."

"What are you thinking?" Mike asks.

"That's Christian," Nic says.

I don't recognize the name, and judging by the confusion in his eyes, Mike doesn't either. "Who?"

"Is there anything else you need, gentlemen?" Michelle interjects. "If not, I need to drop."

"That's all for now, Michelle. Thank you." Nic waves and ends the video call. Then he faces Mike. "Christian Reddick. Tori's brother. Remember? He was up north with his mom when his dad disappeared back in 1991."

Recognition sparks in Mike's eyes. "Ah, yes. Now I'm tracking. Wow. What the hell is his blood doing on the shirt of the sister he didn't know he had?"

"No shit." Nic pauses, forehead creased, tapping the tips of his fingers on the desk. "For all the time I've spent in the Twin Cities over the last few weeks, I have not been able to pin Christian Reddick down and talk to him. Tori says he's basically homeless." Nic blinks as something occurs to him. "Can I use your phone?"

Mike slides his phone across the desk. Nic consults his cellphone for a number, then opens the line on speaker and dials. After a couple of rings the person on the other end answers.

"Hello?" It's a woman's voice, anxious and unsure.

"Hi Tori, it's Nic Morris, Superior PD."

Her tone changes drastically. "Oh, hi Nic! I didn't recognize your number. I almost didn't answer." Her Fargo accent is especially strong, with long, rounded Os and hard Rs.

"I'm glad you did. How are you?"

"Oh, I'm okay," Tori says. "I'm off work today, so Percival and I are just hanging out. We're watching one of those serial killer documentaries on TV."

Nic looks at Mike and mouths the word *cat*. Percival must be the cat's name. "That sounds like a good time."

"How's everything going for you, Nic? Did you find my dad yet?" she asks.

"We're making progress, Tori. I promise. I just can't talk about it quite yet."

"Ooh, okay."

"Listen, Tori, have you heard from or seen your brother since I was last in town?"

"Christian? I —" she pauses. "Yes, he was here just the other day. I was supposed to call you and I completely forgot!"

"It's all right, Tori. How was he?"

"Sick. He said he hadn't had the dope in a couple of days. He kept asking me for money."

"You didn't give it to him, did you?"

"No. He knows that's one of my rules. I think he was just so desperate. He looked terrible, and he smelled terrible, too. He kept going outside to smoke. I think he was hoping that would take the edge off the sickness, you know?"

Nic's eyebrows shoot up. "What did he do with the cigarette butts?"

"He left them in a neat little pile out in my front rock garden." Rustling on the other end as Tori moves around. "I can see them still sitting there."

Mike snaps his fingers triumphantly, and Nic nods in agreement. "Here's what I need you to do, Tori. I'm going to send someone from the Minneapolis Police Department over to get them. Just keep an eye on them until they get there, and don't let anybody touch them. Can you do that for me?"

"Yes. I'm sitting at my kitchen table right in front of the window. I'll stay here until they come."

"Perfect. Thank you," Nic says. "One other thing. Next time your brother shows up at your place, will you call me?"

"Yes. I'm sorry I forgot the last time."

"All good, Tori. All good." Something else occurs to Nic. "By the way, did Christian happen to mention where he's staying right now?"

"Um, no, but he told me that he has a new girlfriend. Her name is Scarlett Jade. Both of those names are colors, did you know that? Scarlet means red and jade is green. I bet Christmas is her favorite holiday."

"I bet it is. Thank you, Tori. It was nice talking to you. And don't forget to call me if Christian turns up."

"I won't forget. Bye, Nic."

"Bye, Tori." Nic hits the button to end the call and looks at Mike. "Scarlett Jade sounds like a stripper name to me," he says with a grin.

Mike chuckles. "Or a hooker."

Nic hits the button again to reopen the phone line. This number he dials from memory. A smoky female voice answers. "Cora Lucero."

"Hey Cora, it's Nic."

"Oh, hey Nic. How's it going?" I wonder if she looks as sexy as she sounds.

"I'm hoping you can do me a favor."

"Of course. Name it."

"Can you send someone over to Victoria Reddick's apartment? She has potential evidence in my Jane Doe case and I need it to be properly collected."

She asks for the pertinent information and tells him she'll take care of it. "What do you want me to do with it once we have it?"

"Send it to Michelle Musgrove at ForenTech Labs in St. Paul." Nic reads the address and phone number from his cellphone. That done, he asks her another question. "Have you ever dealt with a woman named Scarlett Jade?"

"Oh, I know her," Cora says. "She's a well-known addict and prostitute in Minneapolis. Her rap sheet's a mile long. Last I heard she's holed up in a roach motel on the near north side, conducting her business. Why do you ask?"

"Just chasing down a possible lead." Nic glances at Mike and says, "I may be coming back to town here soon. I'll definitely want to talk to her."

"Let me know when you get here and we'll pay her a visit." Nic and Cora say their goodbyes and Nic hangs up.

"It seems another trip to the Twin Cities would be prudent." Mike slides the phone back to its usual place on his desk.

"I mean, somebody has to talk to Christian and his lady friend. Might as well be me."

"Couldn't think of a better man for the job."

Nic stands. "I'll keep you posted." And then he's gone, closing the door behind him.

Mike tries to concentrate on the emails he'd been reading when Nic interrupted him, but he keeps zoning out. Finally he gives up and retrieves his voice recorder from his bag. "Mike Franklin, checking in. Today's date is Thursday, September twelfth, eleven-thirty hours. I think we know who killed Samantha Maines. By some crazy twist of fate, it was her half-brother. That she didn't know she had. For all the years I've been in this job, you'd think I'd have seen it all. Yet the surprises keep coming." He sighs, thinking. "I've been working with a therapist, Dr. Jackie Atkinson, and she's amazing. She's been helping me see and understand my own behavior, even better than the shrinks I had in treatment. We talk about Rachel a lot. She tells me that what Rachel did isn't my fault. She, and she alone, made the terrible decision to do what she did. I'm not sure I quite believe that yet. But we're working through it." Pause. "We talk about Cardinal Doe a lot, too. She says my obsession with this case, and how possessive I am of it, are a direct result of what happened to my wife and daughter. She called it transference, like the Chief did. She says it's also a control thing for me. What Rachel did was one hundred percent beyond my control, so I compensate for that by trying to control everything else in my life. And when the Chief took control of the Cardinal Doe case away from me, well...I took it personally." Another sigh. "I have a tendency to make things all about me all the time, when I should be cheering others on in their success. I mean, Nic is doing awesome work on Cardinal Doe. We're gonna clear our only unidentified person, and that's a win for everybody. I should be happy about that. I'm working on it."

He puts the recorder away and goes back to his emails. I'm super proud of him. For the first time since I've known him, he's truly working on himself.

He just might be okay after all.

PART 3:
THE RIPPLE EFFECT

CHAPTER 22

Mike is out in the bullpen when his desk phone rings. He rushes back in to answer it. "Franklin. Hey, Nic. Hold on, let me close the door and put you on speaker." He does, then sits in his chair. "How's it going in Minneapolis?"

"It's going great, boss. We found Christian Reddick." Nic's disembodied voice sounds a little tinny over the landline. "He was in Scarlett Jade's hotel room, unconscious, breathing erratically. Cora gave him naloxone, and he's coming around now."

"Heroin?"

"That or fentanyl. Probably both." There's a rustle as Nic talks to somebody on his end. "Yeah, load him up and get him to whichever hospital can take him and detox him."

I hear an unintelligible screech in the background, followed by Cora's voice saying, "No, girlfriend, you're going straight to jail."

Nic comes back. "We're transporting Christian to the hospital for detox now. Once he's stable he'll be booked into the Hennepin County Jail. I think I'll be able to talk to him sometime tomorrow."

Mike thinks for a few nanoseconds, then says, "I'll be there."

"You're coming down here?" Nic sounds surprised.

"I am." Mike is resolute.

"Okay. Okay, that's great. Let me know when you get to town and we'll hook up."

"See you soon," Mike says and hits the button to close the line. It rings again right away. "Franklin."

"Hi Mike, it's Michelle Musgrove. Nic tells me he's indisposed at the moment and asked me to call you with my update."

"Yeah, hi Michelle. What do you got?"

"Nic had the MPD send me several cigarette butts for testing. I was able to confirm that all of the butts have the same male DNA on them. Then I compared the profile to the one I developed from the blood on Samantha's shirt. They're a perfect match. Whoever smoked those cigarettes left the blood on the shirt. And he is a male sibling – a full brother – to Victoria Reddick."

"Well, I'll be damned," Mike says, mostly to himself.

"Do you know who it is?" Michelle asks.

"I do. And I never would have if it weren't for your help, Michelle. Thank you."

"Of course," she says.

"I'm headed to the Twin Cities to meet him myself. Nic or I will reach out once we're able to share more detail."

"I would appreciate that. Thank you, Mike."

Mike ends the call and leaves his office for a little while. When he returns he starts gathering up the things he needs for his impromptu trip to Minneapolis: his laptop, a notebook and pen, his digital recorder. To my surprise he also grabs my bracelet and framed sketch. He loads everything into his briefcase and walks out. I follow along above and behind him like a helium balloon on a long ribbon.

"I'm headed to Minneapolis for a couple of days," Mike says to his team as he walks through the bullpen. "Call my cell if you need me."

"Go get 'em boss!" Simon shouts from his desk in the corner. Everyone else laughs and claps as he walks by.

"Smartasses!" Mike calls over his shoulder as he walks down a short hallway and pushes through a set of double glass doors leading outside. He crosses a mostly-empty parking lot surrounded by a high fence.

Wow, the sun is bright. The leaves on the trees rustle in a light wind. Today would be a perfect day for a run. I wish I could feel the warm summer breeze across my bare skin as my feet pound to the beat of my favorite pop songs. Running was more than a sport for me. It was my salvation. When I ran, my mind shut down and my body took over, lungs smoldering, legs propelling me over the uneven terrain of Forest Trails Regional Park. I didn't have to think about my challenging home life with a distant and cruel father and a chronically drunk mother. I didn't have to worry about my sister and whether she would come out the other side unscathed. All I had to do was run.

Somewhere down deep I was convinced that if I ran fast enough, I could make it all better. That's why I always pushed myself to run faster, faster, faster.

Mike uses a key that looks like a mini remote control to unlock the door of an unmarked SUV, then sets his bag on the front passenger seat and climbs in. This vehicle doesn't have all the equipment of a regular patrol car – no siren, no lights, no laptop mounted to the center console. It's just a regular vehicle for higher-level administrators to drive while on duty.

He starts it up and drives out of the lot through a big rolling gate. He takes a left turn onto a busy street lined with bars, coffee shops, banks, gas stations, fast food restaurants, and auto shops. Caribou Creek had a commercial stretch just like this. I think maybe all cities do.

The University of Wisconsin-Superior campus glides by on the right; first a lovely pair of brick monuments marking the entrance, then a long chain-link fence covered in its entirety with an enormous black banner that reads UNIVERSITY OF WISCONSIN SUPERIOR YELLOWJACKETS in giant white letters. It looks to me like this fence marks the boundary of an athletic field. Soccer, maybe?

The commercial district gives way to a residential neighborhood with little parks and older but tidy little houses. When the road ends in a T at Lake Superior, Mike turns right onto another busy street. The lake is on the left and more houses are on the right. He drives a short distance before turning right, and then left, and pulling into the driveway of a lovely old two-story bungalow.

So this is where he lives. And where his wife and daughter died.

Mike gets out of the car and goes inside through the side door, leaving his bag – and me – behind. While he's gone I take in my surroundings.

His house appears to be a Craftsman-style bungalow, with a prominent second-story gable, stucco siding, and wide wood trim. Marley lived in a similar house in Caribou Creek, and I vividly remember the dark wood built-ins, heavy ceiling beams, hardwood floors, and leaded windows. I imagine Mike's house has similar features inside.

Outside the roughly quarter-acre sloped lot is dotted with several fruit trees – crabapple, maybe? – and one giant silver maple in the side yard. The silver-backed leaves that give the tree its name dance in the breeze. The house was built to accommodate the slope, so from the rear it looks like it has three stories instead of two. The basement has a door that opens on a large concrete patio. I imagine that in happier times, Mike might have had a barbecue grill out here, along with a fire pit and some comfy seating. Maybe a table with chairs and a big umbrella for shade. Now it's bare, neglected, and sad. Weeds grow gaily through cracks in the concrete, stretching toward the sun.

I leaned out and looked down…and there she was, lying on the patio, her head cocked at an unnatural angle and a huge pool of blood underneath her. That's what Mike said when he described that particularly awful nightmare. Sure enough, there's a pair of single-hung windows in the second story, directly above the patio. It would have been too easy for a small woman like Rachel Franklin to throw open one of the sashes and launch herself out. Headfirst. After drowning her eighteen-month-old daughter in the bathtub. All while her husband was out picking up dinner.

Mike has never said exactly what happened, but being here and seeing his home, I know. I know I've got it right. I can barely grasp the awfulness of it. I don't know what kind of headspace Rachel must have been in to single-handedly destroy her family and leave her husband in ruins, but it couldn't have been good. No, not at all. And I don't know how Mike makes it through every day after that. It's a miracle he's still among the living.

Here he comes, carrying a smallish black duffel bag. He locks the door behind him, tosses the bag in the back seat of the SUV, and starts it up. We're off to the Twin Cities.

Mike's route takes us back the way we came through Superior, except instead of turning left to head into the commercial district, he follows the Lake Superior shoreline until he reaches the Blatnik Bridge. I think of Jewel and her vehicular homicide case as we ascend the south end of the bridge. Just on the other side of the median barrier is where poor Allie Bergstrom met her untimely end in Jamison Downey's car. At the north end of the bridge is the Rice's Point railyard in Duluth, where Robert Martin froze to death forty years ago.

I will never understand why bad things happen to good people.

Mike navigates onto Interstate 35 and heads south, eventually leaving the cluttered confines of bustling Duluth behind. He sets his cruise control at 72 and settles in for the roughly one hundred and fifty mile drive to Minneapolis.

The scenery between Duluth and the Twin Cities is pretty, but I don't think Mike is admiring it through his mirrored sport sunglasses. I imagine his mind is on me and my case. Maybe he's thinking about what he's going to say to Christian Reddick when he meets him tomorrow.

Honestly, I'm more concerned about what he's going to do.

CHAPTER 23

After a good night's sleep, a shower, and a complimentary hotel breakfast, Mike slings his briefcase bag over his shoulder and walks six blocks to Minneapolis City Hall, a massive Victorian-era granite structure with peaked copper roofs, turrets, and a tall four-faced clock tower. It takes up an entire city block in downtown Minneapolis and houses city council chambers, city offices, and the police department's headquarters. Mike enters the building through a huge arched doorway and crosses the five-story rotunda, headed for the elevator. He stops and rubs the big toe of the Father of Waters sculpture on his way by. The rotunda is cavernous and echoey. The columns and walls and huge staircase are clad in marble. Intricate stained glass windows create a mellow yellow glow that somehow manages to warm the space up.

Mike notices none of this, however. He takes the rickety elevator to the fifth floor and strides down the hall like a man on a mission. He doesn't even stop to peer over the carved marble rail and take in the elevated view of the gorgeous rotunda. Up to this point being in the City Hall building feels like stepping back in time, to when women wore elaborate hats and bustles and men wore tophats and mustaches. That all changes when Mike opens the wooden door with POLICE embossed in gold on the frosted window and steps inside.

The reception area of the Minneapolis Police Department looks remarkably like that of the Superior Police Department on the other side of that door: drab industrial carpeting, white walls, basic office furniture. Not much in the way of natural lighting. Voices talk and phones ring in the background while a uniformed officer behind a clear acrylic barrier that stretches to the ceiling works on a computer. As soon as Mike closes the main door behind him, another opens next to the reception desk and Nic appears.

"Hey, boss, glad you made it. Come on back." He hands Mike a visitor badge to wear while he's here. Mike clips it to his shirt as he follows Nic through a maze of hallways, past offices and a bullpen much like ours. Eventually they reach a short hallway that leads to three interview rooms. Nic enters one and Mike follows him. They sit facing each other across the table, and Mike sets his bag on the floor next to his feet.

"You ready for this?" Nic asks. He has a manila folder in front of him and seems a little anxious.

"I think I've never been so ready for anything in my entire life," Mike says. He vigorously rubs his hands together as if they're cold.

"Cora's bringing him up now," Nic says. Mike nods in acknowledgment.

There's no more small talk from either of them. The moment and the anticipation are too heavy and take up all the space. They pass the time by looking at their phones.

It isn't long before the silence is broken by the jangling of leg chains. Both men look up. A woman in a tailored gray pantsuit walks in through the open door. She is drop-dead gorgeous, with creamy brown skin, full pouty lips painted red, giant brown eyes expertly lined with black, and shiny black hair pulled back into a tight bun. As soon as she speaks I know this is Cora Lucero.

"Right there." She points to an empty chair at the end of the table closest to the door. A large uniformed officer guides a shackled and disheveled man into the room and physically seats him in the chair before going out to the hallway to wait.

The man is wearing an orange jail jumpsuit and white slip-on shoes. His blond hair, probably shaved at one point to hide a growing bald spot, is growing back in uneven patches. He keeps his head down as he sits, leans over, props his elbows on his knees, and stares at the floor.

Cora looks at Mike, and then at Nic. "Hey. You going to introduce us, or what?"

Nic grins. "Cora, this is Captain Mike Franklin. Boss, this is Detective Cora Lucero. She's been a huge help with this investigation."

Mike extends his hand and Cora shakes it. "Nice to meet you," he says. "We appreciate all your help."

Cora waves this away. "It's been my pleasure, Mike." She turns her attention back to the man. "This is Christian Reddick. My understanding is that you two would like to have a little chat with him. Say hello to the nice police officers from out of town, Christian."

"Fuck you." Christian's voice is a deep rasp, as if he'd injured it at some point, or smoked way too many cigarettes. Maybe both. He keeps his eyes on the floor.

"Oh, come on, man. There's no need for the attitude," Nic says. "We just want to ask you some questions. Talk for a little while. That's it."

"I said, fuck you." Christian looks up, and something heavy clamps itself around my throat. Dear god, I can't *breathe*.

∞

I stare through bulging eyes at the face of the man who is literally wringing the life out of me. I don't know him, but I know those eyes. They're my dad's eyes. Panicked, I claw at his hands, trying to dislodge them from my neck. But he holds on tight and squeezes harder.

"You think you're better than me, don't you?" His words drip with unadulterated hate. "Huh? You think you're better than me because your family's still together? Because you have Daddy and I don't? Yeah. Fuck him. And fuck you."

I have no idea what he's talking about. Why did he attack me during my run, drag me kicking and screaming off the trail, and toss me into the back of his rusted out minivan? Why is he hurting me? What did I do? My lungs burst into flames. The pressure in my head is incredible. My vision is going dark around the edges. I try to keep clawing, but my strength is fading. Fast. I'm going to die right here on the nasty floor of this piece of shit van, and nobody will know.

My very last thought before I lose consciousness is of my sister. I'm sorry, Schuyler. I didn't stay safe. I love you too.

I fall into deep, silent, impenetrable darkness. And I stay there for a long time, until this man dumps my body on the forest floor. I have no memory of my life or my death. The trauma is too great to overcome.

∞

Until now. Now I remember everything. The choking sensation eases, replaced by an avalanche of rage and grief that I cannot control. I don't even try. If I could summon the power to destroy Christian Reddick, I would. He destroyed me. He took me away from everyone and everything I loved, and discarded me in the woods like a piece of trash. Raw anguish washes over me in tidal waves. It buries me. I try to scream, directing my vitriol at the man who killed me.

Christian visibly shivers and crosses his arms over his chest. "Damn, it's cold in here. Turn up the heat."

Cora, Nic, and Mike exchange glances. Then Cora says, "Son, the temperature on this floor hasn't been less than seventy-four degrees in…well, ever."

"I'm fucking freezing, man."

It's hard to look at the face of my killer, but I force myself. It's pale, almost gray, and covered in greasy stubble that's starting to turn white around the chin. His green eyes, my father's eyes, are red-rimmed and sunken. His lips are so chapped they're cracked and bleeding in the corners. Years of smoking and drug use have carved deep lines across his forehead, around his eyes, down his cheeks, and at the corners of his mouth. His face tells the story of a difficult life. I almost sort of feel sorry for him.

"All right, I'll leave you fellas alone." Cora backs out through the open door, and it clunks shut behind her.

Nic starts with the administrative stuff for the video cameras and microphones that are recording everything in the room. He reads Christian his rights, and after Christian says he doesn't need a lawyer because he didn't do nothing, Nic moves to the administrative stuff. "Today's date is Thursday, September eighteenth, twenty-twenty-four, nine o'clock A.M. Detective Dominic Morris and Captain Michael Franklin of the Superior, Wisconsin Police Department are here with – can you please state your full name, spell your last name, and state your date of birth, sir?"

Christian rolls his eyes, but complies. When he speaks I notice he's missing a few teeth. "Christian Reid Reddick, R-E-D-D-I-C-K, July second, 1981."

"Thank you," Nic says, then gets straight to the point. "Do you know why you're here, Christian?"

Christian shakes his head. "No idea. Where did you say you were from?"

"Superior, Wisconsin," Nic says.

Recognition sparks in Christian's eyes, and he immediately blinks to try and hide it. Mike, who is watching him very closely, says, "You want to try again?"

"I told you, I have no idea why I'm here, and I got nothing to say to you."

Nic flips his manila folder open and pulls out a print of my tenth grade school photo. Where did he get that? I stare at it, taking in every feature on my face: my easy smile, my sparkling brown eyes, my dark curls cascading over my shoulders and down my back. The bright and vibrant teenager in the photo leaves me feeling unsettled. And, if I'm being honest, more than a little angry. The kid in that photo had such a bright future ahead of her – before her life was snuffed out like a candle.

Nic sets the photo on the table in front of Christian. "Maybe this will help."

Christian's eyes widen. He reaches out with cuffed hands and pulls the photo closer to him, examines it for a few seconds, then pushes it away. "Who's she?" he asks, his raspy voice dripping with insolence.

Nic doesn't react. "She is Samantha Maines. She disappeared from Caribou Creek, Minnesota in August of 2008."

Christian shrugs. "So?"

"So, her decomposed remains were found in Superior nine months later, in April 2009," Nic says.

"Any idea how she ended up dead in my town, Christian?" Mike's blue eyes snap.

"Like I said, I don't know her. Never seen her before in my life."

Nic draws air in between his clenched teeth as he pulls a printout from his folder. "Yeah, see, I've got DNA that says otherwise." He tosses the paper in front of Christian.

"You ain't got DNA that ties me to her or anybody else," Christian snaps. He's paying attention now.

"You might have gotten away with it if you hadn't left some of your blood on her fucking shirt," Mike snaps back. "Let me put this in terms you can understand, Christian: DNA. Doesn't. Lie."

Christian crosses his arms over his chest again and says nothing. He looks remarkably like my dad.

"All right," Mike says. "I bet you recognize this." He reaches into his bag, pulls out my bracelet, and sets it on the table. "That belonged to Samantha. She was wearing it when she died, and it was still on her arm when we found her bones." He leans forward and catches Christian's gaze. "You know what I think, Christian?

I think you know exactly who Samantha is. She's your half-sister by your father. And I think that's why you killed her. As revenge against the man who abandoned your family and started a whole new one."

Christian's face goes white, and for a second I'm sure he's going to pass out. He doesn't, though. Instead he reaches out and touches the bracelet in its case. Several moments go by in complete silence. When Christian finally breaks it, he wants two things: "I want a lawyer. And I want to see my sister Tori."

Mike and Nic stand in unison, gather their things, and leave the room. They walk around a corner and through a door that leads to the observation room. This is a long and narrow room where the surveillance equipment is kept and monitored. A tall metal cabinet holding six receivers with short antennae and lots of blinking lights stands in one corner. A long table holds six computer monitors, one for each interview room. Cora is sitting at one of these. A desk in the back corner, next to the tower, holds a full workstation with enormous monitors that show all six rooms at the same time. Speakers line the walls along the ceiling. It all looks very high-tech. There's also a small table with four chairs. Is this what they do now instead of the two-way mirrors I used to see on my favorite true-crime TV shows?

"He's going to confess," Mike says. "We need to get an attorney and Victoria here ASAP." He sets his bag on a chair and anxiously paces the length of the room.

"I'll call Tori," Nic says, pulling his cellphone out of his pants pocket. To Cora: "Can you send a car to pick her up?"

"Yup," she says, moving toward the door and looking at her own cellphone. "I got someone in the public defender's office who owes me a favor. I'll get him over here now." She leaves the room.

While they do their things, I watch Mike. He takes Cora's seat and stares at Christian on the screen. I can't tell what he's thinking, but I imagine it's something like *THIS is the guy who sent my life into a tailspin fifteen years ago?* Either that, or *I can't believe we finally got him.* Maybe both.

Nic hangs up with Tori and immediately makes another call. "Jim, hey, it's Nic Morris. Listen, I'm calling with an update on Samantha Maines. I'm in Minneapolis and we're talking to the guy we think kidnapped and killed her." Pause. "Yeah, it's pretty ironclad. We have DNA." Pause. "An upstanding citizen named Christian Reddick. He's her half-brother." Pause. "They have the same father. You know him as Daniel Maines." Pause. "Yes. Yep, I know it. Listen, I'll come see you when we're done here, and I'll bring everything I have with me. Video, reports, everything. I think this is going to end up being your case to prosecute." Pause. "Great, I'll see you this afternoon." He ends the call and goes over to Mike. "You okay, boss?"

Mike, who is still watching Christian Reddick intently, nods. "Yeah. Yeah, I'm okay." He sighs deeply. "I don't know. All these years I've wondered how she died, and now that I'm about to find out I'm not sure I really want to know."

Nic nods. "I get it. Sometimes ignorance really is bliss." He puts a hand on Mike's shoulder. "You can stay back here if you want to."

"I think I will. I don't trust myself to keep a cool head."

Cora enters and sits in a chair next to Mike. "I'll hang out here with you. We'll have our own little watch party and watch Nic work his magic." She points at Nic. "Lawyer and Tori should be here within the hour."

Nic finds a chair and everyone looks at their phone to help pass the time. I think about the cellphone I had when I died; it looked nothing like the handheld touchscreen computers they have now. Mine was smaller and boxier, had a tiny LCD screen and push buttons. I could send text messages, but it took a long time to type them and they cost like a dime apiece. Now they can write texts using their voices. I remember leaving my phone in my car when I went for my final run because I didn't want to carry it. I wonder if things would have turned out differently if I'd had it with me.

It isn't long before the uniformed officer who brought Christian into the interrogation room pokes his head in. "Cora, they're here. Waiting for you in reception."

She jumps up and strides out, and returns with a nervous-looking Victoria Reddick. A tall bearded man wearing navy blue pants and a blue button-down shirt with the sleeves rolled follows, but he doesn't come into the observation room. He veers off and goes straight to Christian's interrogation room, where he can be heard on the speakers introducing himself as public defender Seth McMillan and telling Christian that his blanket advice is to "shut your mouth and say nothing at all."

Christian's reply: "I want to see my sister."

Nic stands and goes to Victoria. "Thanks for coming, Tori."

I can see the family resemblance between Christian and Victoria. She's quite a bit younger than he is, quite a bit shorter, and quite a bit rounder. Her limp blonde hair falls to her shoulders. She wears black flowy capri-length pants, a white vneck t-shirt with food stains across her ample breasts, and cheap flip-flop sandals. She clutches her nylon purse to her abdomen and looks at Nic with wide eyes. "What's going on, Nic?"

Nic guides her to a chair at the smaller table. She sits, and he takes the chair next to hers. "I'm sorry I couldn't give you more information over the phone," Nic says. "But we have Christian in custody. We found him yesterday with Scarlett Jade, actively overdosing."

Tears fill Tori's wide green eyes and spill down her cheeks.

Nic takes her hand. "He's all right. We gave him naloxone and got him to the hospital to detox."

Tori's other hand flies to her lips. "Oh, thank goodness."

"Here's the thing, Tori. We believe Christian may have been involved in the disappearance of a teenage girl up in Caribou Creek back in 2008."

Tori frowns. "What do you mean?"

Nic takes a deep breath. "In April 2009 the skeletal remains of a young female were found in Superior, Wisconsin. They weren't able to identify her then, and she stayed unidentified for fifteen years. Now, thanks to new DNA technology, we know who she is and we're getting closer to finding out what happened to her. And we believe Christian is involved."

Tori blinks, her long eyelashes still wet from crying. Her demeanor suddenly changes from shock and surprise to…anger? No, scratch that. What I see in her eyes is absolute fury. "What did he do, Nic? What in the heck did my brother do?"

"I think he wants to be the one to tell you," Nic says. "We have him in the next room and he wants to see you."

Tori's jaw muscles work as she stands and follows Nic to the interrogation room, where Christian and Sam are waiting.

Cora scoots her chair closer to Mike so they can watch on the computer screen. I watch too.

Nic and Tori enter the interrogation room. They sit in chairs on the opposite side of the table, facing Christian and his attorney.

Christian breaks into tears. Tori's face is stone cold.

"All right," Nic says. "You've got what you asked for. Let's talk."

Christian wipes his face with his shackled hands and looks at his sister. "I fucked up, Tori."

"You've been fracking up your entire life," Tori points out with zero trace of any emotion. I believe she has surpassed the limits of empathy for her brother. "What did you do to that girl?"

Christian hangs his head. Seth reminds him that his advice is to say nothing. Another moment or two pass, and Christian says in a low voice, "He left us and started a whole new family."

Tori leans over the table in an effort to hear him. "What? Who did?"

When Christian looks up again, his eyes are blazing. "Dad did!" he shouts.

Tori sits up, taken aback. Her eyes are wide.

"All right, calm down," Seth says, a warning edge in his voice.

"He left us —" Christian points at Tori and then himself "— and Mom, and he got himself a new name, a new wife, a new fucking family."

"But—but how do you know that?" Tori asks.

"I saw him on TV, Tori. Back in like 2007, he won some kind of fucking award for his job and he was on the news. He looked exactly the same, except older. His name wasn't Reid Reddick, though. It was Daniel Maines. So it took me a while to figure it out."

Tori just stares at her brother, wide-eyed.

"I wanted to talk to him, you know? I just wanted to know why he left us. Why he left me. I thought maybe we could be a family again." Christian's raspy voice catches in his throat. "So I tracked him down at his office, you know, that was pretty easy, and then I followed him home. I—uh, I don't know what I expected, but it wasn't a big, beautiful home, a beautiful young wife, and two beautiful daughters. I didn't expect that." Tears spill from his eyes and roll down his cheeks. "He had this perfect life, while you and me grew up stuck in a piece of shit trailer with that fucker Tom Kline."

Nic pauses his note-taking to interject. "Your stepfather, right?"

"Our kiddie-diddling asshole stepfather," Christian confirms.

"He's very abusive," Tori says. "The regular kind and the sex kind."

"Did you confront your father?" Nic asks.

Christian shakes his head. "No. I chickened out. But I was so pissed, I started thinking about ways to get back at him for what he did to me. To us. It was all I could think about for days and days. I spent hours on the computers at the library, learning everything I could about his new family."

"How did you choose Samantha?" Nic asks. "Why take your revenge on her? She was innocent."

"Because she's almost exactly the same age as Tori," Christian looks at his sister with haunted eyes. "Tori was born in August

1991, and Samantha was born in December. That meant my dad was fucking around on my mom even before he left."

Nic blows air out through his lips and writes this down.

"So I started following Samantha. Watching her, waiting for the right time."

This triggers another memory, this one awash in dread and vague fear.

∞

When given the choice to run indoors or outdoors during the summer, I will usually choose outdoors. I like the fresh air and the sunshine, and the terrain at Forest Trails Park is far more challenging than a treadmill.

Except when it rains. Some runners don't mind running in the rain, but I can't stand being wet. My clothes get heavy and clingy, my shoes squish when they make contact with the ground, and my hair plasters to my neck. I feel like I'm suffocating. On those days I go to the gym and run on the boring treadmill.

This is one of those days. The sky is gray and gloomy. Rain falls in sheets, creating rivers in the gutters and lakes in the potholes. Definitely a gym-running day. I drive to Haven Fitness, the gym where my mom has worked as a personal trainer for many years, and find just two open parking spaces. Both are easily visible from the front window, where the treadmills are situated. This is good. Thefts from cars are a well-known problem at all the gyms in the area, and I like to be able to keep an eye on my car while I run. I park my car in one of those spaces and book it inside.

I wave at Jeanette, the front desk attendant, and stick my head in the owner's office. "Hey, Pat."

Pat Lennox looks up from his computer and smiles. He's an easygoing man with a quick smile and way more muscles than most men in their sixties. "Hey, Sami, how are you today?"

"I'll be better after I finish my run. The weather sucks today."

"Can't argue with you there. Enjoy your run."

I wave and head to the fitness floor. My route takes me past the weights area, where muscleheads grunt and clank and drop heavy things on the rubber-covered floor, then walk around making sure everyone sees their muscles getting bigger. I roll my eyes and beeline for the treadmills. There's one open. It's busy here today.

I'm just hitting my stride, music pumping through my earbuds, when I notice a beat-up old minivan with rusting panels turn into the parking lot. It looks totally out of place here, at an expensive gym. I watch as it slowly cruises up and down the drive lanes, then carefully pulls into the spot next to my car. Its headlights shine directly on me, blinding me and making it impossible to see who's behind the wheel.

Nobody gets out of the car. The headlights stay on, rain slicing through the beams like shards of glass, and the wipers rhythmically sweep water off the windshield. What is this person doing? Are they coming in or not? I wish they would turn those damn lights off.

They don't. The van sits there like that for several minutes. A strange, uneasy feeling forms in my gut: is this guy watching me?

I'm not alone; the women on either side of me suddenly end their workouts and scurry away.

I keep up my pace and wait to see if the minivan moves or leaves now that the two women have left. I mean, he could be here to pick someone up.

Nope. He doesn't move. At all.

The bottom falls out of my stomach and chills run up and down my spine. It's me he's watching. It has to be; there's nobody else visible through the window but me. I hit the kill switch on my machine and step off, then head straight for Pat Lennox's office.

"That was qui—" He interrupts himself when he gets a good look at my face. "What's wrong, Sami?"

"There's a creepy van in the parking lot, and I-I think he was watching me." My hands and my voice shake uncontrollably.

In my brief experience, some men would brush me off and tell me nobody's out there watching me, stop being so dramatic. My dad, for one. Pat Lennox is not some men, or my dad, and I love him for it. He immediately stands and hurries to the front door. He cracks it open and peers out, ignoring the deluge soaking his head. My heart chatters in my chest. I don't think I've ever been so scared in my life.

Pat steps back inside long enough to grab the umbrella Jeanette has for him, then goes out into the monsoon and marches up to the minivan. I hide behind a treadmill and watch through the window as he speaks animatedly to the driver, the umbrella-less hand waving and pointing. He stands back as the minivan reverses out of the spot and drives away. Sweet relief washes over me, and my hands slowly stop shaking.

Pat comes back inside, soaked through in spite of his umbrella. "He's gone."

"Did he say what he was doing?" Jeanette asks.

"He said he was waiting to pick somebody up. I told him I know all of my customers personally and asked for a name. He couldn't give me one. So I told him he had fifteen seconds to get the hell off my property before I call the cops."

"Thank you." My whole body is shaking now, releasing tension.

"Of course, Sami. You're welcome. I want all of my guests to feel safe here."

"I would hug you, but —" I gesture at his wet clothes with an ironic grin. He chuckles. "That's okay. Next time."

I decide to abandon my run and just go home. During the drive I glance in my rearview mirror and see a familiar pair of headlights slicing through the rain.

My god, is he following me?

∞

It turns out he was; I was abducted and killed just days after the incident at the gym.

"You were waiting for the right time to…what?" Nic asks.

Christian shrugs.

Nic frowns. "You didn't know?"

"Not really. All I knew was I was gonna grab her. And I did, when she went for a run in that park. It was easy to hide, and she never saw me comin."

It's true. I didn't.

∞

It's a beautiful day, the rain is gone and the sun is shining, and I'm about halfway through my run at Forest Trails Park. I'm well into the zone, my heart pumping, my lungs expanding and contracting as my feet pound along the paved path. Music blasts through my earbuds, and I don't hear or see him sneak up on me. It doesn't occur to me until it's far too late that I probably should have taken some safety precautions, especially after the creepy minivan at the gym incident.

He attacks me from my right side, strong arms wrapping tightly around me and lifting me right off my feet. He smells like sweat and cigarettes. I kick, thrash, and scream, all to no avail. Both of my earbuds fall out and get lost in the underbrush.

"Shut up," he hisses. "Shut the fuck up or I will fucking kill you."

Where is everyone? Can't they hear me? The arms keep me locked tight as he carries me out of the woods. The familiar minivan is parked on a residential street at the edge of the park, just a few dozen feet from the trail, and its side door is open. He literally throws me in, and I land in a mess of fast food wrappers, empty cigarette packs, half-full cans of pop being used as ashtrays. The van reeks of stale cigarettes and marijuana. He climbs in behind me and slides the door shut. Then he wrestles me onto my back and climbs on top of me, sitting on my abdomen and pinning my arms to my sides with his legs. It isn't hard for him to do; he probably has twelve inches and fifty pounds on me.

∞

"Did you know you were going to kill her?" Nic asks.

Christian shakes his head. "Not until I had her in my van. She wouldn't stop screaming and crying. Asking me what I wanted and not to hurt her."

∞

"Please," I sob. "Please, don't hurt me." Terror floods my incapacitated body. My heart pounds in my throat. My charm bracelet is stuck between his knee and my arm, and it digs painfully into my skin.

The eyes looking back at me are black with anger…but also familiar somehow. I blink. They look like my dad's eyes. How is that possible?

"Do you know who I am, bitch?"

"N-no," I stammer.

He leans down until his nose nearly touches mine. The sour rot of his breath makes me gag just before his warm hands clamp around my neck, cutting off my airway. "You think you're better than me, don't you?" His words drip with unadulterated hate. "Huh? You think you're better than me because your family's still together? Because you have Daddy and I don't? Yeah. Fuck him. And fuck you."

My fingers desperately claw at his hands. Oh god, I can't breathe.

"Guess what, sweetheart. He was my daddy first." With that he leans his entire body weight on his hands.

The last thing I feel before I lose consciousness is the sharp crack of my airway collapsing.

∞

"It took a long time for her to die." Christian's voice is devoid of emotion. "My nose started bleeding, I was working so hard."

"And that's how your blood ended up on her shirt," Nic says.

"I guess."

"What did you do after she died?"

"I didn't know what to do. I just drove around until I could think of something. Hours and hours I drove. I ended up in Duluth somehow. Decided to cross over to Superior and leave her there. I figured it would take a while for Wisconsin and Minnesota cops to figure it all out."

"It took fifteen fucking years," Mike mutters. His ears burn a bright red.

Christian is quiet for a long time. Then he says, "I thought punishing my dad for what he did would make me feel better. But that ain't what happened. Every time I close my eyes I see the life leaving that girl's eyes. Still. To this day." He looks at Victoria. "You always ask me why I do drugs. Well, now you know why. It's the only way I can make Samantha's face go away."

"You almost died yesterday, Christian," Nic points out.

Christian shrugs. "I don't give a fuck if I die. One less fucking failure for the world to deal with."

Mike entire body jerks violently at this, surprising Cora. "You okay, Mike?"

"Uh. Yeah, I'm fine." He clears his throat. "Sorry, didn't mean to startle you."

Suddenly I'm sure: Mike has been where Christian is. He's felt like a failure who's no good to anybody. And I'd bet my bracelet he's thought long and hard about not being in this crazy, fucked up world anymore. *One less fucking failure.*

Tori bursts into tears. "What about me, Christian? Huh? Did it ever occur to you that *you* are all *I* have? And now I'm going to be all alone." Her sobs take on a high-pitched whistling sound as she breathes in. "How could you hurt that poor girl? Our sister! You're so fracking *selfish*!"

Christian covers his face with his shackled hands. "I'm sorry, Tori. I'm so sorry." His words are muffled, but the regret and the anguish are clear in his voice.

Cora stands and tells Mike, "I think we've heard enough. I'll grab Officer Dunbarton and take Christian back to his holding cell."

Mike nods. "Good idea."

While Cora does that, Nic guides Tori back into the observation room. They sit at the table again and Nic waits patiently while Tori composes herself. When her sobs finally subside, leaving her with hiccups, she looks at Nic and asks, "Where is my father now?"

"He lives in Caribou Creek," Nic says.

Tori thinks about this for a moment. "And I have another sister?"

Nic nods. "Her name is Schuyler."

"I'd like to meet her."

"That can be arranged," Nic says. "I may need your help one more time, Tori. Would you be okay with that?"

Tori nods vigorously. "Anything."

"Okay. Okay, great. I'm going to have an officer take you home now, but I'll call you later today with the plan, all right?"

Tori agrees.

Mike stands and stretches. "I'm going to head back to my hotel, see if I can't get a few more Zs." He looks like he needs them.

"Sounds good, boss. I'll keep you posted."

Mike slings his bag over his shoulder, says his goodbyes, and makes his way back to his hotel. He keeps his eyes on the ground as he walks, deep in thought.

Once he's safely tucked away in his room, Mike finally lets go of all composure. He sits on the edge of the bed, covers his face with his hands, and cries. He cries like I've never seen him cry; the sobs border on hysterical and seem to come from some deep, untouchable place within him. I imagine he's crying for me and how long it took to finally bring me justice. Maybe he's crying for his lost wife and daughter. Or for himself, and all of his wasted years. I wonder if, now that the Cardinal Doe case is finally coming to an end, he's becoming unstuck and cleansing his soul in preparation for the next phase of his life.

Mike lies back and, fully dressed, clutching a pillow to his chest, he curls into the fetal position. The sobs start to trail off into hitching breaths. His breathing slowly gets deeper and more regular.

And then he's asleep.

CHAPTER 24

The light outside Mike's hotel room window is growing dim when his cellphone rings, startling him awake. He smacks the bed all around him looking for the phone before realizing it's in his pocket. Eyes still closed, he fishes it out and opens the line. "Franklin." He clears his froggy throat. "Yeah, hey Nic." Pause. "Wow, okay. What time is it now?" His eyes pop open. They're still red and puffy from falling asleep while crying. "Seven-thirty? Are you serious?" He groans. "I did not mean to sleep this long." Pause. "Okay, so what did Detective Gardiner have to say?" He listens for a long time. "I bet he did. What's the plan now?" He listens for quite a while, then: "Sounds good. I'll drive. Text me your address and Tori's, and I'll pick you both up. Be ready to go at oh-eight-hundred hours." Pause, then a small smile. "I appreciate the invite, but I'm going to stay in. Probably just grab a sandwich from the deli across the street. You and Cora enjoy your dinner." He ends the call and plugs his phone in to charge.

Mike must not be very hungry, because he does not grab food. Instead he takes a long shower, comes out wearing just boxer shorts, and climbs back into bed. He uses the remote to turn on the TV, but it isn't long before he turns it off again, buries himself under the covers, and goes back to sleep.

He doesn't wake again until the sun comes up the next morning.

CHAPTER 25

Mike is up bright and early, rested and refreshed. He must be feeling pretty good; he even smiles at the barista as he places his order for two black dark roast coffees and one vanilla latte at the coffeeshop in the hotel lobby. He carries them to his SUV and heads out to pick Nic and Tori up.

Nic is staying at his cousin's house on the far north side of Minneapolis. He's sitting on the front step of a tidy stucco Cape Cod with black awnings over the windows and a tiny patch of green lawn when Mike pulls up to the curb. When Nic opens the door, I can hear rumbles and screeches somewhere nearby.

"Trains." Nic buckles his seatbelt and gratefully accepts the coffee Mike hands him. "There's a big trainyard a block and a half down, where the street ends. Those damn things are constantly moving and making a shit ton of noise. Other than that the neighborhood's great. Tanner has awesome neighbors and no problems at all."

Mike looks around. "I'll admit, this isn't the Minneapolis one expects to see after watching the news."

"You only ever hear about the bad shit," Nic says. "There's way more good shit that happens here, but you don't hear about that. Fear is what attracts the eyeballs, and therefore ad revenue."

Mike nods. "Fair enough."

Nic directs Mike to Tori's house on the northeast side of town. A giant bridge carries us over Interstate 94, a double set of train tracks, and the Mississippi River. Mike navigates narrow, congested streets and oblivious bicyclists until he finally pulls up in front of an old two-story L-shaped house that's been divided into a duplex.

"Be right back," Nic gets out of the car and takes the latte with him. The front door opens as he walks up the path, and Tori steps out. She's perfectly dressed for a family reunion in a floral print dress and brown sandals. She smiles when Nic gives her the coffee, and they make their way to the car.

"Hi Tori," Mike says as Tori climbs into the backseat and buckles her seatbelt. Nic does the same in the front passenger seat.

"Hello." She takes a sip. "Thank you for the coffee."

"My pleasure." He puts the car in gear and pulls away from the curb, then doubles back the way he came and gets on the interstate heading west. There isn't a lot of small talk as the suburbs of Minneapolis and their big box stores, chain restaurants, office buildings, and car dealerships fly by outside.

Mike exits the interstate and onto another highway, which takes us straight north through even more suburbia. It feels familiar to me. Comfortable. Like I've been here before and it's where I belong. Eventually I spy a green sign that says **Caribou Creek Pop. 27,300**.

A completely new sense of calm familiarity settles over me. I know this place. I'm home.

Mike takes us through Caribou Creek's quaint downtown with its historic brick buildings lining a narrow main street. A large fountain, which also doubles as a splash pad for the kids, has pride of place right in the center, next to the Mississippi River. My mom would bring Schuyler and me here to play in the water all the time when we were little, then take us for malts at the diner down the block.

Those were fun days.

Mike turns into the parking lot of a squat, glass-faced building a couple blocks down from the fountain. The sign out front confirms that we have finally reached the Caribou Creek Police Department. Mike leads the way to the front door. Nic falls back a bit to walk with Tori, who is moving slowly so as not to spill her coffee.

Inside the heavy glass doors is a reception area. Chairs are lined up neatly against the block walls like toy soldiers. A civilian receptionist sits behind a bulletproof window in the far wall. Next to the window is a heavy steel door.

The receptionist, a middle-aged woman with bright, inquisitive eyes and a lovely smile, watches Mike approach the window. "Hi, you must be Captain Franklin."

Mike agrees that he is and shows her his ID. "I have Detective Dominic Morris and Miss Victoria Reddick here with me." Both show her their IDs as well; I notice that Tori has a basic state identification card and not a driver's license. Like a typical suburban teenager, I can't imagine not driving. I wonder if she takes the bus.

The receptionist stands, grabs something off her desk, and opens the door. She hands a day pass to everyone as they file by.

"Jim is waiting for you in Interview Two. It's the middle door over there." She points.

Mike thanks her and we head in that direction. Detective James Gardiner stands to shake everyone's hand as they enter. He's a large, top-heavy man with unruly gray-brown hair and a bushy mustache. His hands look strong, with fingers like sausages. He wears a gray CCPD polo shirt roughly the size of a sail and khaki pants belted below his overhanging belly. This room has a big two-way mirror like normal interrogation rooms. "Nice to see you all," he growls, but in a friendly way. "Thanks for coming."

Everyone sits around the table. Mike places his bag on the floor next to his feet. "So what's the plan?"

Nic gestures to Detective Gardiner, who says, "I have Kimberly and Schuyler Maines waiting in Interview One next door. I figure Schuyler and Victoria can hang out here and chat, and then I guess we decide where we go from there."

My mom and my sister are both here, and I get to see them. My heart soars.

"I'd like to speak with Kimberly at some point," Mike says.

Gardiner nods. "That'll be no problem."

Nic looks at Tori. "Are you ready?"

Tori folds her shaking hands on the table in front of her and looks at Nic with wide, anxious eyes. "Ready as I'm ever gonna be."

Gardiner stands. It takes some effort to heft all that weight, but he manages. "All right, I'll go get her."

Mike stands and follows him out. "The observation room is around the corner," Gardiner says as he ambles to the next room on widely-spaced legs. Mike thanks him and goes there. This room is much smaller than the one in Minneapolis, and although there is recording equipment, it also features three one-way windows. There's a speaker mounted above each window, with a switch that turns it on or off and a dial for adjusting volume. Several chairs are scattered around the narrow room. Mike pulls one up to the middle window and settles in to watch.

"Mind if I join you?" I know that voice. It's my mother's voice. She's standing in the doorway watching Mike anxiously. Her long, curly hair was the color of coffee when I last saw her, like mine and Sky's. Now it's mostly the color of steel. I'm shocked by how much she has aged in sixteen years. The skin on her face and her neck hangs, her mascara-caked eyes are sunken, and her brow seems to be set in a perma-scowl. She used to be fit, with a body any woman would kill for. Now she's just skinny. Too skinny. I think I can see every joint in her hands, and her fitness tracker, buckled as tightly as possible, hangs from her bony wrist.

Time – and wine, I'm sure – have not treated my mother kindly. God, I just want to hug her.

Mike gestures to a chair next to him. "Please do."

She sits and gives Mike a smile. There she is, the younger Mom I remember. "Thanks. I'm Kimberly Maines. Schuyler's mom."

"And Samantha's mom," Mike says, and smiles back, shaving years off his own face. Two smiles in one day? He must really be feeling better. "Mike Franklin. Superior PD."

My mom chuckles softly. "Right." She pauses, then says, "Listen, I want to thank you for everything you've done for Sami. Jim told us how hard you worked to identify her all these years."

Mike shrugs awkwardly and his ears turn pink. "Oh, you're welcome. I'm sorry it took so long."

"What did you do with her remains?"

"We buried her in a beautiful plot at Nemadji Cemetery in Superior. She has a headstone, a gorgeous sugar maple tree, and a great view of the river."

This brings tears to my mom's eyes. "Oh, that's so wonderful. Thank you."

They exchange another glance, then Mike clears his throat. "What do you say we turn it up and listen in?" He reaches for the dial and twists it counterclockwise, and they both watch through the mirror.

Nic is in the middle of introductions. "--sorry that you had to meet under these circumstances," he says. "I'm sure it was a shock to both of you to learn you had additional siblings out there."

Sky and Tori both nod, then glance shyly at each other.

My mom sighs deeply.

"Detective Gardiner and I are going to step out and give you some privacy, but we're not going far. Just holler if you need us."

Sky and Tori watch them leave. I don't know where they go, but they don't join Mike and my mom in the observation room.

Sky and Tori sit in silence for an uncomfortably long time, stealing looks at each other, unsure how to start the conversation. Tori's big green eyes are wet with nervous tears. I can tell she wants to say something, but doesn't know what. Sky is also emotional, which manifests in busy hands. Her polished nails, probably acrylic because as a youngster she was *obsessed* with press-on nails, go *tik-tik-tik* on the tabletop.

Of the two, I expect Sky will be the one to break the ice, and eventually she proves me right. She suddenly sits up straight, gives Tori a frank look, and says, "You and Sami have the same eyes. Dad's eyes."

She's right, of course. The only difference is that mine were brown and Tori's are green. But the round, slightly downturned shape is identical to our father's eyes. Christian has them too.

It's like Sky's words break a dam wide open and the words just start pouring out of both of them.

"I've never seen a picture of him," Tori says.

"You haven't?" Sky is utterly appalled by this revelation.

Tori shakes her head. "My mom had him declared dead in 1995, when I was four years old. After that my stepdad made her throw everything that was his away. All the things from their marriage, too."

Sky pulls her phone from her purse and scrolls through the photo gallery. She selects one and shows it to Tori. "That's him."

Tori gasps. "My gosh, he looks just like Christian!" She gazes at the photo for so long that Sky gently sets the phone on the table so she doesn't have to hold it anymore. "I see the eyes," she whispers.

"Does he look like you imagined?"

"Sort of. I always thought he was taller. And had more hair."

This makes Sky laugh.

Tori finally, reluctantly, slides Sky's phone back to her. "I wasn't born yet when my dad left, so I never knew what life was like with him around. My brother, though…he really suffered. Still does."

"Thus how we find ourselves here today." Sky frowns. "It's not fair, you know? One man, our father, makes one stupid decision, and all of us are paying for it. Christian didn't deserve to be abandoned. Sami didn't deserve to die. You and I didn't deserve to lose our siblings." Her voice quavers a bit.

Tori nods. Tears leak from her eyes. "It's not all bad, though."

"What do you mean?"

A nervous chuckle escapes Tori. "I have a sister! I thought I was going to be alone forever."

This makes Sky cry too, and she reaches across the table, hands open, inviting Tori to take them. She does.

Mike turns the volume down and looks at my mom. "Can I ask you a question?"

My mom turns toward Mike. Her legs are crossed. She's so thin she can easily hook her top foot behind her bottom leg. "Sure."

"How did you meet your husband?"

My mom looks down at her lap, then back up at Mike, as if she was expecting the question. "Well, I'm sure you know by now that I used to be a personal trainer."

Mike nods.

"I started working at Haven Fitness in River Junction – that's where I'm from – when I was still in high school. I worked my way up from washing towels to concierge to teaching fitness classes, and I finally became a personal trainer. Pat Lennox, the gym's owner, was really supportive. I worked my tail off, and it wasn't long before I was the most sought-after trainer he had. I had a lot of longtime, repeat clients, and I made Pat a ton of money over the years.

"My schedule was usually booked out for days. Weeks. But one day in 1990, I believe it was October, a client canceled and a new name showed up on my appointment book: Daniel Maines."

"Had you ever seen him before?" Mike asks.

My mom shakes her head. "Never."

I know what Mike's thinking: in October 1990 Daniel Maines was still Reid Reddick and living in Minneapolis with his wife Susan and son Christian. Why would he join a gym in River Junction, twenty miles away, under a different name?

Elementary, my dear Watson. He did that because by then he was already planning to leave.

"Our relationship was strictly professional at first. But he started coming two or three times a week, and we really got to know each other."

Mike's eyebrows go up. "Wow, that's a lot of time to spend with a trainer. And money. What time of day did he usually come?"

"He always came in the middle of the day. Between noon and two o'clock." Mom says. "Daniel isn't a conventionally handsome man, but his charisma more than made up for it. I found him to be charming and funny. He made me laugh all the time. It got to the point where I really looked forward to our sessions because he made them so fun."

"Charming," "funny," and "laugh" are not words that I would ever associate with my father. He was running a scam, even back then.

"Did he ever talk about his personal life?"

Mom thinks about this for a long moment. "He never did. And I never asked. I respected his boundaries. But I also noticed that he wasn't wearing a ring."

"And eventually…"

Mom sighs and nods. "Yeah, eventually we crossed the line. What a cliché, huh? Fucking the personal trainer."

My mom so casually dropping a cuss word like that would have made me blush if I were alive. She always tried to avoid them. I guess a lot of things change sixteen years after a deeply traumatic experience like your kid's disappearance.

"Where did you have your trysts? Right there at the gym?"

Mom shakes her head. "I had a townhouse in Caribou Creek. We just started meeting there rather than at the gym for our 'sessions'." She used her bony fingers to make air quotes.
"When did things get serious?" Mike asks.

"He moved in with me in May of 1991. I was already pregnant by then, and we got married in July. Samantha was born in December."

"Did you know much about him by the time you got married?"

A deep sigh from my mother. "I mean, he still never talked about his life before me, except that he was an only child and both of his parents were gone. I also knew he worked in investments. All I really knew was that he loved me, and he was funny and charming and sensitive. I thought that was enough. But then everything changed when Samantha was born."

"What happened?"

She shrugs. "Some switch somewhere flipped, and my husband was suddenly an entirely different person. Jealous. Controlling. Manipulative. A narcissist."

Susan Kline, Dad's first wife, had said something very similar.

"The girls' lives, and mine, have always been tightly controlled. He put cameras up inside and outside the house. I found a tracking device on my car, and one on Sami's not long before she disappeared. He always has to know where we're going and who we're with. And the things he says to break us down, just really horrible, wretched things." She pauses for a long time, thinking. "I suppose now, looking back, I know why he needs to keep the girls and me in line. He has secrets and will do anything to protect them. Anything." Mom's eyebrows draw together and she blinks hard. "Even forbidding us to look for Samantha after she went missing." She sighs. "This is going to sound terrible, but for a long time I thought he didn't want to look for Samantha because she was the only one of us who ever stood up to him. He hated that. A few times I even wondered if he did something to her."

"Did you say anything to Detective Gardiner about your suspicions?"

My mom shakes her head. "And risk Daniel's wrath? No. I didn't."

Mike says nothing, and they sit quietly for awhile. Then he turns the volume up on the interview room's speaker again.

"I want to confront him," Tori says. Her eyes, dry now, are blazing.

Sky's eyes widen. "I don't know if that's such a good idea…" The fear and self-doubt, planted and nurtured by our asshole father, creep into her voice. "I mean, what if he–"

"What can he do to us? We'd be here, in the police station. Wouldn't we? Nic?"

Nic must have been listening from somewhere else, because he magically appears at the door at just the right time. Jim Gardiner is right behind him. "I think it's a great idea."

Mike stands and holds a hand out to Mom. "Come on, let's join the party."

She allows him to help her up, and they make their way back to the interview room. Mike carries his bag in one hand, and sets it on the floor when he finds a chair at the table. He introduces himself to Schuyler before he sits.

"The man you know as Daniel Maines has left a trail of wreckage in his wake over the last forty years, maybe more," Nic says. "You all know he left his first family, took a new name, and started a second one." He gestures to Tori and Sky, and also my mom. "But what you don't know is, he stole the Daniel Maines identity from a client's dead son to avoid getting caught for stealing obscene amounts of money from his clients."

"We think there's a good chance he's stealing from his current clients as well," Mike adds.

"Oh, god," my mom moans, and covers her face with her hands.

Sky blinks as something occurs to her, then she looks at Mom with huge eyes. "The Florida house."

Mom shakes her head, but says nothing.

Sky turns her attention to Nic. "He just told us over the weekend that he bought a winter home in South Florida. Showed us pictures of what's actually a beachside mansion. Says it's his 'retirement plan.'"

Nic turns to Mom. "Were you involved in that transaction, Mrs. Maines?"

"No. I thought he was attending a conference in Atlanta."

"I wondered how he could afford a multimillion-dollar house in Florida, but I didn't dare ask and wreck his good mood," Sky says.

Nic looks around the room. "The FBI has had a warrant out for his arrest since 1991. He's hurt a lot of people. It's time he's held accountable."

"So what do we do?" Tori asks.

They huddle around the interview room table and sketch out their plan. That done, Jim Gardiner leads the group back out to the reception area.

Nic shakes his hand. "Thanks, Jim. We'll see you tomorrow."

"Can't wait." He looks like he means it, too. He waves and disappears as the door clunks shut behind him.

Sky and Tori embrace. "See you tomorrow," Tori says. Sky waves and she and my mom walk away. I wish I could go with them. More than anything.

Tori, Mike, and Nic climb into the SPD vehicle and buckle up for the forty-five-minute drive back to Minneapolis. Nobody talks. There's too much to think about. Mike drops Tori off at her house with a promise to be back at eight o'clock sharp the next morning. Then he takes Nic back to his cousin's house. He pulls up to the curb and throws the SUV into park. "We're almost there, aren't we?" His voice is low and heavy with emotion.

Nic nods. "Yeah." He looks at Mike, his baby blues brimming with sympathy. "Yeah, we are. How are you feeling with all this, boss?"

Mike sighs. "I honestly don't know, Nic. Cardinal Doe has been a monkey on my back for so long that I can't even fathom what my life will be like without her. You know? I have no goddamn clue. What am I supposed to do with that?"

I know what he means. What will closing the case mean for me? Will Mike and Nic give my bracelet back to my mom and my sister? As much as I would love to hang out with them forever, the fact of the matter is I'm still dead. I can't help but wonder if I'll ever have the chance to leave the land of the living and go wherever the souls of dead people go.

Nic surprises me again with his unexpected wisdom. "Well, I guess this is your chance to make your life what you want it to be."

Mike watches a young boy on a bike slowly crossing the street half a block down and contemplates this. "But…what is that?" He says this mostly to himself. "I don't even know."

"You will," Nic puts a hand on Mike's shoulder and squeezes, then pushes his door open. "You will, boss."

Then he's gone, walking up the front walk toward the house.

CHAPTER 26

Mike is silent during the drive back to his hotel. When he's finally back in his room, he sits on the end of his neatly made bed and pulls his voice recorder out of his bag. "Mike Franklin, checking in. Today is Thursday, September nineteenth, and–" He glances at his wrist and finds that it's bare. "–I have no idea what time it is. I'm in Minneapolis for what looks to be the long-awaited conclusion of the Cardinal Doe case." He pauses, thinking. "I told Nic when I dropped him off that this case has been a monkey on my back for so long that I have no idea how to do life without it. I know it seems weird, to be so thoroughly attached to a case, but…" Pause. "But it's the truth. This case nearly destroyed me, and then it became my salvation." Pause. "Nic said this is my chance to make my life what I want it to be. Wise kid. Question is, what is that? Answer is, I have no idea. I've never put a single moment's thought into what I want my life to be. I didn't think it mattered, especially after I lost Rachel and Kylie. I've been stuck in the how it *is*.

"I really am thrilled that we know who Cardinal Doe is now. I'm happy that we brought her home. And tomorrow I'll be over the fucking moon to hold the man who ultimately caused her death accountable. Oh, Reid Reddick, Daniel Maines, whatever you want to call him, he didn't personally kill his daughter Samantha. He didn't want her dead, and maybe he even loved her. But the choices he made decades ago eventually led to her death. It's a ripple effect. One action, no matter how big or small, creates a series of other actions that impacts everything they touch. Just like when a raindrop falls into a pool. Or a bathtub."

Mike lowers the recorder to his lap and sits in silence for a long time. Then: "I have experienced the ripple effect myself, you know. I don't talk about it because the shame I carry with me every minute of every day won't allow it." He takes a deep breath. "Well, today I'm going to take Jackie's advice and defy that shame. I don't want to carry the burden anymore. I'm going to speak my truth."

What could Mike possibly have to be ashamed of?

"May twelfth, 2005. That's the day my wife Rachel drowned our daughter in the bathtub and then jumped out a second-story window, killing herself. I didn't kill them, I was across town picking up dinner when it all went down. But my selfishness and pride make me every bit as culpable as Rachel is. Maybe more so. No matter what Jackie Atkinson says, I'll probably always feel responsible.

"You see, her pregnancy with Kylie was difficult, and she suffered serious postpartum depression after birth. Rachel was in such bad shape that she couldn't get out of bed, couldn't stop crying. She was so completely convinced she was a terrible mother that she just stopped trying. She couldn't bond with Kylie and couldn't take care of her. I never left Kylie alone with her during those first few weeks.

"We were very fortunate to have a fantastic OB-GYN who immediately recognized the signs at our six-week checkup and referred Rachel to a psychiatrist in Duluth. Over the next several months Dr. Pacey worked to get Rachel stabilized. And, with the right medications and the right therapist, she came back better than before. She ended up being a fantastic mom and we were finally a happy family. I was so proud of her for battling back."

Mike takes a few deep, calming breaths, then continues. "We agreed not to have any more kids. But you know, time has a way of dulling even the most vibrant memories. We were in a good place for a long time, and it became easier to forget or dismiss the dark times. Right around Kylie's first birthday I decided I wanted her to have a sibling. Rachel was completely recovered, she's working with a shrink, what are the chances of that happening again? That was my rationale, anyway. It all made perfect sense in my head.

"Rachel was absolutely opposed to the idea. She tearfully asked me why I wanted to put her through that again, and isn't the one we have enough?" Pause. "It should have been. But it wasn't. I couldn't let it go. Somehow having another baby became more important to me than my wife's health and my family's safety. I kept pushing, kept pressuring her until she finally said okay, we'll give it a try. We got pregnant almost immediately." Mike takes another, shakier breath. "When I saw the positive pregnancy test, I was triumphant. I felt like I had won. As if this was some kind of fucking competition."

A mirthless chuckle escapes him. "The joke was on me. Rachel miscarried at six weeks. I was devastated. She seemed relieved. I hated her for that." Mike's whole face crumples and his voice cracks. "And she knew it. Three weeks later she and Kylie were dead." A long, agonized pause, and then: "I guess she won in the end, didn't she?"

He turns off the recorder, lays back on the bed, and sighs. "I'm sorry, Rachel," he says softly to the empty room. "God, I'm so sorry for being a pigheaded asshole. You deserved so much better than me."

Mike doesn't completely break down like he did after describing his "Why I dead, Daddy?" dream, but he's visibly emotional. Tears roll over his temples and soak into the bedspread.

I am absolutely flabbergasted. I suspected the murder/suicide, but I had no idea there was so much more to the story. Of course he feels guilty and ashamed; he believes he caused their deaths because he insisted on trying for another baby.

The ripple effect.

He lies prone on his bed, hands clasped over his midsection, and stares at the ceiling until his cellphone rings. "Franklin." He sits up. "Hey Nic." He listens for a moment. "Sure, it's in my bag. I –" Pause. "Oh, okay. Awesome idea." Pause. "Sounds good. See you in the morning."

He stands and stretches, then moves to the room's tiny desk, pulls his laptop out of his bag, and spends the evening working. He breaks only for dinner, a sandwich and fries from a nearby restaurant. I wonder if it's as good as Stewie's pastrami on rye. The digital clock on the bedside table says 10:41 when he finally shuts his computer down and goes to bed.

He already seems…better. Lighter. Like the weight of the world has been lifted from his shoulders.

I guess confessing to a ghost will do that for a man.

CHAPTER 27

Mike pulls up to the curb and Nic hops in, carrying a blue reusable shopping bag in the crook of his arm. "Did you bring it?"

"Yeah, it's in my bag."

"Sweet."

Mike pulls away from the curb and starts the journey across the river to Tori's house. "You're really looking forward to fucking with his head, aren't you?"

"It will be my absolute pleasure." Nic settles into his seat and grins. His lovely blue eyes are extra sparkly this morning.

They pick Tori up and make the long drive up to Caribou Creek. There isn't a lot of conversation, but the anticipation is palpable.

Tori nervously wrings her hands in her lap. "I'm glad Sky will be there with me," she says when Nic asks how she's feeling.

Jim Gardiner is waiting in the vestibule when Mike, Nic, and Tori walk in. "Good morning," he rumbles. "You ready for a show?"

Nic claps his hands. "Let's do this."

Gardiner opens the heavy steel door and leads everyone to the interview rooms. Schuyler and my mom are already sitting in Interview Two. Sky looks as nervous as Tori does. I get it. She's never stood up to our dad. She was always the peacekeeper, never one to rock the boat or get in trouble.

"I made the call," Gardiner says. "He'll be here in a few minutes."

"Then there's no time to waste," Nic says. He has Sky and Tori sit next to each other along the far side of the table, facing the door. Then he pulls from his blue bag two eight-by-ten framed photos. The first is a blown up print of Christian Reddick's booking photo. Nic places this on the table next to Tori. The second is my tenth grade school photo. This he sets next to Sky, then gestures to Mike, who hands Nic the framed Cardinal Doe sketch from his bag. Nic sets this next to my school picture. Then he backs up to take it all in and declares it perfect.

I agree. It's a chilling scene: all of his kids from both of his families are represented, and Reid Reddick/Daniel Maines will have to answer to them. Like Nic, I can't wait to see his face when he realizes the gig is up, and he no longer has secrets to keep. It's going to rock his world.

"Jim," a voice travels across the room from the front desk. "He's here."

"Be right back." Gardiner lumbers toward the vestibule door. Mike smiles at my mom. "Care to join me in the observation room?"

She smiles back. "I would love to."

He holds the door open for her, then they take the same chairs they occupied yesterday. "You ready for this?" Mike asks.

My mom puts her hands together like she's going to pray, then presses them against her lips. "I don't think so."

Nic comes in and sits between them, then jumps to standing. "Here we go."

The interview room door opens, and Gardiner points to a chair. My dad sits. Gardiner leaves without a word, closing the door behind him.

I'm shocked at my dad's appearance. I thought my mom had aged a lot in sixteen years; she's got nothing on my dad. He's…well, he's shriveled. Just a whisper of the scary and intimidating man I remember. His goatee and what's left of the hair on his head are pure white. His basic green t-shirt and blue jeans hang on his wasted frame. His arms are bony, his joints knobby, and his upper back is hunched. He looks like an old man.

I have to remind myself that he is an old man. My dad is supposed to be sixty-nine years old, but Nic had said that Reid Reddick is well into his seventies now. He looks every single one of those years.

His eyes, though…they're still bright and clear and as shrewd as ever behind his rimless glasses. And they are taking in the scene before him with confusion.

"Schuyler? What's the meaning of this?" His voice is old, too. Tight and raspy.

Sky takes a deep breath, then takes Tori's hand in her own. "Dad, I'd like to introduce you to someone."

My dad gives Tori the up and down. He doesn't recognize her at all. I guess he wouldn't; she was still in the womb when he left his first family.

"This is Victoria Reddick. My sister."

It takes a few seconds for my dad to understand. As comprehension dawns in his eyes, his wrinkled face goes white and he covers his mouth with his hand. His eyes dart from the photos to his daughters and back again to the photos.

Nic leaves the observation room, and he and Gardiner appear in the interview room. Gardiner sits in an empty chair, but Nic paces the room. "What do you think, Reid?"

My dad visibly flinches, but says nothing.

"It's official, our Cardinal Doe is your daughter, Samantha Louise Maines. The DNA Kimberly and Schuyler gave us proves it."

My dad crosses his arms over his chest and scowls.

"You want to know what else their DNA tells us, Reid?"

"My name is Daniel Maines." My dad's teeth are clenched tight.

"Samantha was killed by her half brother." Nic picks up Christian's mugshot and sets it on the table directly in front of my dad. "That would be your son, Christian Reddick."

For a second I think my dad is going to pass out. Gardiner must think so, too, because he gets up and stands behind Dad's chair.

Nic pretends to see none of this. "Christian abducted Samantha while she was running in Forest Trails Park. Then he strangled her to death and dumped her body in Superior for us to find nine months later. Why would he do that, Reid?"

My dad's eyes are fixed on Christian's mugshot. I imagine it's a little like looking in a mirror. The resemblance is that strong.

"He did that for revenge. Because he found out that you didn't just go missing back in 1991. You very intentionally abandoned your family, changed your identity, and started a whole new life. And a whole new family."

Tori's and Sky's faces are both streaked with tears. In the observation room, a strangled sob escapes my mom. I can only imagine how hurt and betrayed she feels. She was duped right along with everyone else.

"All of this subterfuge, these lies, all the hurt and pain you've caused – and for what? All to hide the fact that you'd been stealing your clients' money for years."

My dad finally manages to speak. "That's bullshit."

Nic stops next to my dad and leans over to make eye contact. "To the tune of several million dollars, Reid. That's a lot of ching, and sure helps finance a nice lifestyle." Nic stands and resumes pacing. "But your firm caught on. And so did the FBI. So you had to disappear. And you stole your clients' dead son's identity to do it."

"Bastard," my mom mutters.

"Are you stealing from your clients now, too?" Gardiner's voice is even more growly than usual. "I'm sure the FBI would be very interested to hear what you've been up to. In fact, did you know that arrest warrants don't expire? They've had one out for you for thirty-three years. That's gotta be some kind of record."

My dad throws Gardiner a look that could probably kill a small animal. "Fuck you. Fuck all of you. I want my lawyer."

That is Nic's and Jim's cue to end the interview, and they leave the room. My mom stands and storms out of the observation room. Through the window I watch her storm into the interview room and sit in the chair recently vacated by Detective Gardiner. I've never seen her so angry. Ever.

The color falls out of my dad's face again, but the defiant glare stays on.

"Are you proud of yourself, Daniel?" She shakes her head hard. "Reid. Whatever the hell your name is. You've destroyed two families. And for what? A little money?"

"You don't know what the fuck you're talking about, Kim. You have no fucking idea."

"God, I feel so stupid." My mom's throat works as she fights to control herself. "I believed you, Daniel. I believed everything you said. And to find out it's all a lie, I just –" Her voice hitches, and she stands. "I hope you rot in hell for what you've done." She looks at Sky and Tori. "Come on, girls. Let's leave your dad alone with his thoughts."

They gather up the framed photos and leave the room. They pass Mike outside the observation room; he's on his way to have his turn with my dad. The bracelet in its acrylic case is in his pants pocket.

The interview room door opens just as Mike reaches out to turn the doorknob. My dad is surprised to see Mike there, blocking his exit. "Get out of my way."

"We're not done with you yet, Mr. Reddick." Mike, who has four inches and probably sixty pounds on my dad, steps forward and forces him back inside. "Have a seat."

"I will not sit and listen to these outrageous lies any longer. I'm leaving."

Mike takes hold of my dad's upper arm and carefully but forcefully makes him sit. "You're not free to leave. And I'd like to call out for everyone listening that since you asked for an attorney, this is no longer an interview. I won't be asking you any questions. I'm simply taking the opportunity as a civilian, not as law enforcement, to make sure you understand the extent of the damage your behavior has caused over the years. Are we clear on that?"

My dad crosses his arms again and says nothing.

"My name is Mike Franklin. I'm Captain of the Investigations unit at the Superior Police Department." He pulls the bracelet from his pocket and tosses it on the table in front of my dad. "This was basically all that was left of your daughter when we found her. This bracelet and some fucking bones."

My dad hunches into himself.

"You know, I had a family once. A lovely wife and a beautiful little girl. I lost them when my wife had a postpartum psychotic break. She killed my daughter and herself, and I was alone. No more family to love and take care of and protect. Your daughter Samantha came along not too long after that, and I became obsessed with giving her her name back. When I failed, I had a breakdown of my own. Samantha has haunted me every single day for fifteen years as I've tried to learn how to live life without my family.

"And here you are, fortunate enough to have had *two* families, and, intentional or not, your selfish choices destroyed both. You have to live with that now, Mr. Reddick. I hope the money and the lifestyle were worth it. Because there's a special place in hell for people like you."

Mike takes the bracelet back and signals toward the mirror. Nic and Gardiner are there within seconds. Nic yanks my dad to his feet and Gardiner places him in handcuffs while reading him his rights. "I'll be right back," he growls. "Just gotta take out the trash." He pushes my dad out the door and they disappear.

Everyone else gathers in the interview room and sits around the table. Nobody speaks for a long time, but most everyone dabs their eyes at least once. Mike holds the acrylic case containing my charm bracelet and gazes at it contemplatively. Then he does something I've never seen him do in all the time I've been with him: he pops the case open and removes the bracelet. Then he turns to Sky, who happens to be sitting next to him. Her wet eyes widen.

"Back in 2009 I made a promise to myself and to Samantha that I would not rest until I gave her back her name and delivered her to her family." He clears his throat and blinks back tears. "Now that we've done that, I want to give this to you." He lays the bracelet on his palm and holds it out to Sky.

She bursts into tears. "Thank you," she sobs. "Thank you so much." She picks it up and slides it on her right arm – and something suddenly shifts within and around me. I feel different. Like I'm floating. There's another force pulling me, beckoning me, telling me it's time.

With my baby sister taking possession of my bracelet, the tether keeping me here is almost broken. I understand now. I'll be going home soon.

Jim Gardiner returns and joins the party around the interview room table. If he notices the tears in everyone's eyes, he doesn't show it. "The Reddick and Maines women may be asked to provide additional information as the prosecution of Reid Reddick progresses." Mom, Sky, and Victoria all nod in unison. Gardiner turns to face Tori. "Your mother may also be approached for questioning. You may want to let her know what's all happened here."

Tori nods resolutely. "I haven't spoken to my mom in almost twenty years. I suppose this is as good a reason as any to reach out. We'll see if she'll talk to me."

"Cora can help if you need it, Tori," Nic offers.

She looks at him gratefully. "Thank you, Nic. But you know, I'm going to give it a try on my own. I might just be okay."

Nic gives her an encouraging smile.

"Gentlemen, thank you." My mom's face is a mess of smeared eye makeup, but she's somehow smiling. "We've had to learn some unpleasant truths over the last couple of days, and we'll have to figure out a way to move forward. And we will." She looks at Sky, then at Nic, then at Mike, and finally at Jim Gardiner. "Thank you for showing us who Daniel Maines really is and holding him accountable for what he's done. But most importantly, thank you for bringing Samantha home." Her voice breaks on my name and tears fill her eyes again.

The sensation of weightlessness intensifies.

When Sky stands up and goes around the room giving hugs to the detectives, I realize I'm moving with her now, and not with Mike. When Sky leaves the Caribou Creek Police Department, I'll never see him again.

The thought makes me profoundly sad. And when I look at his face, I see the sadness in his eyes, too. His albatross case is finally solved, but in the end he lost his anchor. I hope he can find a way to move on without me. If anyone deserves to have a good life, it's Mike.

God, I'll miss him.

I follow behind Sky as she and Mom and Tori walk arm-in-arm out into the bright late summer sunshine. Tori stops and looks shyly at Sky. "Um, could I call you sometimes?"

Schuyler throws her arms around Tori and pulls her into a tight hug. "Oh my god, yes," she says fiercely, her eyes brimming with tears. "Call me anytime. Call me all the time. We're sisters."

My mom smiles, tears in her own eyes.

With that, the last tiny gossamer thread holding me to this earth finally breaks. I can go knowing who I am, how I lived, how I died, and that my family is going to be okay. I can go knowing that Mike Franklin, the man who never, ever gave up on me, is going to be okay. I can go knowing my life, and my death, mattered.

I blow my sister Schuyler one last kiss as I leave her.

She turns her face to the sun and smiles.

THE END

ACKNOWLEDGMENTS

My undying gratitude goes out to all of my family, friends and colleagues who have offered kind and supportive words throughout my journey. And to my readers, without whom none of this would be possible.

Thank you.

ABOUT THE AUTHOR

Brenda Lyne is the pseudonym of author Jennifer DeVries. Jennifer lives just outside Minneapolis, Minnesota with her two busy teenagers and two furbabies. She is living, breathing proof that it is never too late to follow your dreams. *Ripple Effect* is her sixth novel.

ALSO AVAILABLE FROM BRENDA LYNE:

Raegan O'Rourke teams up with Jesse Hendricks, police officer and aspiring detective, to investigate the case of a missing mother and her baby.

But when her family's feud with the evil Fausts escalates, can she solve the case – **and** protect her family?

BOOK CLUB
DISCUSSION QUESTIONS

Character & Emotion

How does Mike Franklin's personal grief shape his investigation of Cardinal Doe's case? Do you think he's driven more by guilt, justice, or something else?

Cardinal Doe is both a ghost and a narrator—how does her perspective affect your connection to the mystery and the people trying to solve it?

What emotional parallels exist between Mike's trauma and Cardinal Doe's search for identity? How do they reflect and heal each other?

Mystery & Revelation

Were you surprised by the identity of Cardinal Doe and the truth behind her murder? What clues did you pick up on (or miss)?

How does the use of forensic genealogy affect the pacing and tone of the story? Did it feel realistic and believable to you?

The case takes 15 years to solve. What do you think kept the story emotionally gripping during that time jump?

Paranormal & Symbolism

The charm bracelet plays a significant symbolic role in the story. What do you think it represents for both Samantha and Mike?

How does the ghost element enhance or shift the emotional impact of the story compared to a traditional murder mystery?

Samantha remains tethered to Mike for 15 years. What does this say about the unfinished business of the dead—and the living?

Family & Consequences

What themes about family legacy and generational trauma emerge as the truth behind Cardinal Doe's life unfolds?

What does Ripple Effect say about the consequences of one person's choices on generations of others? Who do you think caused the first "ripple"?

The Reddick family and the Maines family were both shattered by Reid's actions. How does the book explore the cost of running from the past?

Personal Reflection

If you were in Mike's position, would you have reopened the case despite being told not to? Why or why not?

Do you believe in the idea that spirits linger for a reason? How did this story impact your beliefs about life after death?

What would justice have looked like for Samantha—was it achieved by the end?